"There's a lot to like in Jose[...] [...] [...] *Cutting Cards Of Death*: Mystery, romance, intrigue, history, snappy dialogue, and even a heartfelt love letter to Paris and North Carolina's Outer Banks. A great beach read, in more ways than one!"
—Richard Helms, Derringer and Thriller Award-Winning Author of *Brittle Karma*

Undertow of Vengeance, Joseph Terrell's fourth thriller in the Harrison Weaver crime writer series, and set in North Carolina's Outer Banks, is a knockout. With the deadpan savvy delivery of Humphrey Bogart as Sam Spade and the clipped declarative sentences of Dashiell Hammett, this volume, like its predecessors, reaches out in the very first sentence, grabs you by the lapels, and never lets up.
—Joseph Bathanti, former North Carolina Poet Laureate

Smooth writing from an eloquent storyteller goes down like fine scotch. *Undertow of Vengeance* is a keeper.
—Maggie Toussaint, Author, Cleopatra Jones Mysteries

"Every once in a while I'll pick up a book and from the first sentence, I'm engaged. Written with an extraordinary eye for detail yet in the sparse language of the journalist he once was, Terrell's novel is filled with wonderful dialogue, believable characters and just enough plot twists to keep the reader turning pages."
—Kip Tabb, Freelance Writer, former Ed. *North Beach Sun*

"Joe Terrell gets the Outer Banks just right, from crashing surf to the sordid crimes behind the tourism façade, to a thoughtful sleuth who can throw a punch and make a mean sweet tea."
—David Healey, Author, *The House That Went Down With The Ship*

"A smart, savvy combination of who-done-it and police procedural."
—Kathryn R. Wall, Author, the Bay Tanner Mysteries

Calling Cards of Death

A HARRISON WEAVER MYSTERY

JOSEPH L.S. TERRELL

BellaRosaBooks

BellaRosaBooks

CALLING CARDS OF DEATH
ISBN 978-1-62268-153-2

First Printed: June 2020

Also available as e-book: ISBN 978-1-62268-154-9

Printed in the United States of America on acid-free paper

Cover design by Roo Harris
Author photograph by Lynne Scott Constantine

Book design by Bella Rosa Books

BellaRosaBooks and logo are trademarks of Bella Rosa Books

10   9   8   7   6   5   4   3   2   1

This book is dedicated to independent bookstores everywhere, and especially to Jamie Hope Anderson of Downtown Books and Duck's Cottage; Bill Rickman of Island Bookstores; Venetia Huffman of Read 'em and Weep; Gee Gee Rosell of Buxton Village Books; and to Brian Spence, Abbey Bookshop, Paris, France.

Author's Note:

This is a work of fiction, and although I have used an occasional name of a real person, all of the main characters are purely figments of my imagination. Most of the places mentioned are real, but as I have done in the past, I've compressed time to use the Dare County Courthouse as it used to be used—to house the sheriff's department as well as other county offices. I want to extend thanks to retired FBI agent Larry Likar for his insight into the behavior of psychotic killers. Appreciation is also due first readers Veronica Moschetti Reich and Kathy Kelly for their editorial suggestions and catches; and especially to professional concept editor and talented author Beth Terrell, who worked tirelessly with me to make this a better story. Also, once again, my deepest appreciation to Rod Hunter, publisher of Bella Rosa Books, for his faith in me as a writer.

–JLST

Calling Cards of Death

Chapter One

A parakeet lay on the steps leading up to my little blue house, feathers ruffled, small feet stiff and curled. The same bright yellow and green coloration as my Janey.

I sucked in my breath and my heart beat faster.

"My, god, how did she . . ." I raced to the steps, picked up the bird and cupped it gently in my hand. Its head lolled to one side, and I caught a glimpse of its face. I felt a flood of relief.

It was not Janey.

The little leathery patch at the bird's nostrils was blue. A male. My Janey, like all mature female parakeets, has a beige leathery patch.

Saddened for the little bird, I took a closer look. Its neck appeared to be broken. The way its head twisted to one side.

Intentionally killed?

I was convinced of it.

Someone had done this act of cruelty with malicious intent. Meanness. Deliberate evilness. And it was a message. A message left on my stairway, and a bird to look like my Janey. The act gave me a chill of dread; but anger swelled up too.

A few days earlier when I stepped outside just after dawn, I had found three half-smoked cigarette butts at the end of my driveway, just behind my Subaru. Neither of my two neighbors smoked. Someone had stood outside my house at night at least long enough to partially smoke three cigarettes and leave them there on the ground for me to see. It was a deliberate act. I was sure of that.

I had picked up the butts. Kools. I didn't even know Kools were made any longer, but it was a brand I had smoked years ago before I quit cigarettes. I trashed them.

Now these two things, coupled with an incident last week, began to fit together.

My name is Harrison Weaver. I'm a crime writer. After working many years in the Washington area, I moved to North Carolina's Outer Banks, those windy, narrow barrier islands that stretch a hundred miles down the state's coast-line. At the north, there's Kitty Hawk just across the bridge linking Currituck County, then Kill Devil Hills, Nags Head, and on down across Oregon Inlet to Hatteras Island and by ferry to Ocracoke Island.

As a crime writer, I'm accustomed to pulling together what appear to be disjoined occurrences that, when viewed together, make a picture. And there was a picture emerging in my mind.

Someone was letting me know they were watching.

That first piece of the picture came last week at Barrier Island Bagels in Market Place in Southern Shores. I had gone there in midmorning after I finished some writing and planned to sit outside at my usual round table. As I went in to order my cinnamon-burst bagel and small black coffee, I noticed a book lying open but face down on the table as if someone had accidentally left it there. No food or coffee cups were on the table. Just the book.

Placing my order, I told Sas, the muscular young man behind the counter, someone had left a book on the table. He shrugged, said a guy had sat there earlier without ordering anything. Enjoying the sunshine, he added, scurrying about with my order and probably several others.

I took my coffee and bagel—lightly toasted with very light butter—outside to the table, settled in and looked more closely at the book. It was a dog-eared paperback copy of Hemingway's short stories. Since there was no owner's name inside, it was another book I would treasure, even though I've got at least two of copies of the collection. Hemingway, the hero of my youth.

I took a bite of my bagel, wiped my fingers, and absently turned the book over to see where the reader had left off. It was the title page of the fine short story "Hills Like White Elephants." It was one of my favorites, and I had even used it in several talks on writing I'd given. It was a prime example of Hemingway's theory that a writer doesn't need to give all of the details of a story; readers get pleasure out of being able to fill in and come to realize some of what lies below ten percent of an iceberg that shows above the surface.

Deceptively simple, the story occurs with conversation between a man and a woman at a small hot and dusty train station, and it deals with pregnancy and abortion, although neither is ever mentioned. And those hills that look like white elephants can be symbols of the woman's soon-to-be swelling belly.

Now, finding that book as if planted at what was customarily my table, and the cigarette butts, and the dead parakeet, I knew this was too graphic to be random. It had to be planted, planned.

I realized I was frowning in thought as I took the poor little parakeet and a small shovel and gave him a decent burial underneath the large live oak tree in the vacant lot beside my house.

I could no longer ignore these acts. Someone wanted my attention. But who? And why?

I couldn't help it. I felt a tug of dread.

Chapter Two

Trudging up the outside stairway, I unlocked the door and stepped into the dinette and kitchen area. My parakeet, Janey, chirped a head-bobbing greeting to me. I went to her cage and put my hand inside. She hopped up on my finger and then off again. With my index finger, I touched her breast and rubbed her head. She nibbled at my finger and chirped some more. "Yes, Janey, I'm happy, very happy, to see you again, too."

I meant it, and I thought about the little parakeet I had just buried, its neck broken, and the same coloration as Janey. Someone had taken pains to select a parakeet that looked like Janey; and someone was familiar with the cigarette brand I used to smoke; and someone knew I had used the Hemingway story in talks.

It was all vaguely scary.

I wanted to talk with someone about this, and of course the person I thought of right away was my long-time friend SBI Agent T. (for Thomas) Ballsford Twiddy, who his friends all called "Balls." He was a tough, no-nonsense guy, and one hell of a good investigator. He and I went back many years to when I was starting out as an investigative newspaper reporter. By a series of fortunate clues that fell my way, I was able to lend him help early on in solving an exasperatingly tangled crime. Since that time he had called me his lucky charm and permitted me to tag after him from time to time.

He knew I could keep my mouth shut when necessary and only write about a case when it was safe to do so.

After speaking with Janey and breathing easy that she was all right, I went across the living room to my landline and plopped down in the chair beside the phone.

I took a few deep breaths, in through my nose, out through my mouth. Checked the time. Five minutes to eleven a.m. I punched in Balls' cell phone.

He picked up on the third ring. "Yeah?"

"You busy?"

"Course I'm busy." I heard some noise in the background as if he had moved a bucket or something. "Cleaning my car."

He referred to his vintage Thunderbird, the love of his life. Well, except for his wife Lorraine and two grown children.

"I was just going to run something by you," I said.

"You haven't found another body down there at the Outer Banks, have you?" Balls lived near Elizabeth City, about forty-five miles from me at Kill Devil Hills.

"Nope, no dead body, but . . ."

"Well, then let me get back to my automobile."

"Balls," I said, "I think I'm being stalked."

There was a pause on his end of the line. It sounded like he put a bucket down. I could almost picture him, frowning slightly, leaning a hip against the shiny fender of his beloved car. "Whadda you mean?"

I told him about the parakeet that I thought at first was Janey, and the cigarette butts, and book of short stories. He made that humphf sound he does from time to time. "You been reading too many detective stories," he said. "Or writing 'em." Even though his comments were flippant, there was something about his tone that signaled me he was taking what I said more seriously than his words conveyed.

"I'm serious," I said, although I didn't really need to say that. He knew me well enough to know I was concerned.

Another pause. "I gotta be in Manteo in the morning, meet with Sheriff Albright and Chief Deputy Odell Wright.

Afterwards, maybe lunch?"

"Yes."

"You're buying," he said.

"As usual." Then, "What are you working on with the sheriff and Odell?"

"None of your damn business."

That was his standard banter. I'd find out later, and he knew it.

"We'll talk about your imaginary stalker at lunch." He chuckled, but there was little mirth in the sound. "Looks like maybe you've really pissed somebody off."

"Yes, that's what I'm thinking."

Chapter Three

After Balls and I signed off, I remained sitting for a few minutes, then got up and slid the glass door back and stepped out on the deck into the warm sunshine. I tried not to think about the string of incidences that signaled someone wanted my attention, and instead I looked at the sky and breathed in the light breeze off the ocean, only a quarter of a mile or so away. I always felt I could smell the faintly salt air off the ocean. I breathed in again.

The late August and early September days were some of the best. Locals and tourists alike monitored the weather channels with dedication this time of year, as we were well into the hurricane season. A couple of tropical depressions lurked out in the Atlantic off the coast of Africa. Maybe they wouldn't amount to a threat here on our coast. Weather forecasters were sounding a bit excited about one of the depressions that had formed into a tropical storm named Dora. Fingers crossed.

I went inside and brought the handset of the phone out onto the deck, took a seat on one of my deck chairs and called Elly. It was just before her lunchtime, and I figured I could catch her before she left to go home for lunch, or outside, or maybe even ate at the courthouse where she worked.

Elly—her first name is really Ellen—Pedersen is my sweetheart. We've been seeing each other for close to three years now. She works at the Register of Deeds office. Elly is a widow with a son, Martin, who has started kindergarten this year. Except for when his birthday occurred, he could almost be in the first grade.

I called her work number. One of her co-workers, Becky, answered and announced to Elly in a teasing, sing-song voice, that someone special was on the phone.

When Elly came on the phone, I said, "Hello, this is someone special."

A soft musical laugh at her end of the line. "Yes, it is."

"Thought I'd just check with you before you went to lunch."

"Yes, going to dash home today for lunch. Martin is off today because of some sort of planning session at school. I'll join him for a quick lunch. And Mother."

Elly lives with her mother in a several-times-remodeled Sears home from the 1930s, near the Manteo airport. Just ten minutes or so from the courthouse.

"See you tomorrow night?" I said.

"That sounds good," she said.

"I'll be in Manteo at lunchtime tomorrow, but I'll be meeting Agent Twiddy."

I know her well enough to know she had cocked one eyebrow questioningly. "Something up, Mr. Crime Writer?"

"Oh, no, just catching up with him"

"Um-huh," she said, not believing me at all.

I didn't want to talk with her about my suspicions, certainly not yet. She had almost become reconciled to the fact that I made my living writing about murder and mayhem; in fact a few cases were right here at the Outer Banks, and she had been dangerously close to a couple of them during the investigations.

The next morning, a little after eleven o'clock, I checked on Janey's food supply and water, and actually locked my door as I left. I didn't always lock it, but had decided I really needed to.

Traffic was a bit heavy as I headed south on the Bypass, or Highway 158. We call it the Bypass although actually it bypasses nothing—with the exception of the Atlantic Ocean, and not even the ocean following a truly vigorous northeastern storm or hurricane. Businesses and restaurants cluttered each side of its five lanes. The Beach Road, Highway 12, to the east and parallel with the Bypass, is the only other north-south road on this section of the Outer Banks.

I moved over to the far right lane toward Whalebone Junction and swung right toward Manteo, the county seat of Dare County. Manteo is located on Roanoke Island, where the ill-fated Lost Colony attempted to be the first permanent English settlement in 1587.

Crossing Roanoke Sound on the high-rising bridge, I looked down at the sprawling clusters of apartments at Pirates Cove and the handsome boats gleaming white in the sun at the marina. One small boat left a V-shaped wake as it headed toward the bridge.

Another swing to the right after the bridge and I was on the road into downtown Manteo. I passed the Christmas Shop and Darrell's Restaurant and turned right at the light at Sir Walter Raleigh Street. Probably find a parking place up close to the courthouse. The old brick courthouse—built in 1904, a year after the Wright Brothers' historic flight—squats at the end of Sir Walter Raleigh and Budleigh streets, and dominates the downtown, despite the mushrooming cafés, galleries, and shops that have increased each year it seems.

I lucked out with a parking space across the street from Jamie's Downtown Books, one of my favorite places. Checking the time, I stuck my head in the bookstore to say hello—and breathe in the heady aroma of new books. Jamie wasn't in. She was probably up at Duck's Cottage in Duck, where she's the book buyer.

Twenty-something-year-old Evans was behind the counter, minding store. I spoke to him and asked how he'd done in the tryouts for a role in an upcoming performance by the Theater of Dare. "I'm thrilled," he said, with a flourish of his hands. "I got the role of Biff. Just the one I wanted."

"Break a leg," I said.

"Oh, thank you," he said, grinning like the whole world was bright and shiny.

I went around to the front of the courthouse and the comfortable low steps to the porch. Elly's office is just inside the front porch on the left. Going inside, I saw Elly talking with a paralegal from one of the attorney's office. Elly had one of the large, heavy deed books out on the counter between them. She saw me and gave a little smile and a slight nod of her head and went back to business.

Taking the stairs, I headed up toward Sheriff Albright's office. I met Mabel coming out of the sheriff's office. She wore a loose top that came down to her hips, and her black soft-soled shoes, which favored her sore and swollen ankles. Mabel had been with the sheriff's office for a hundred years or more, and through the tenure of at least two sheriffs before Albright. She had told me earlier that she was never going on another diet. Hell with it, she'd said, or words to that effect.

She smiled at me.

I grinned.

"If you're looking for Agent Twiddy," she said, "he's in the sheriff's office with Odell." She carried a thin brown folder in one hand. "But I think they're winding up."

The sheriff's door opened with Balls still saying something back to the sheriff. Chief Deputy Odell Wright waited beside Balls, and then the two of them came out into the hall. They left the sheriff's office door open.

Odell nodded at the office next to the sheriff's and started toward it but stopped to speak to me.

Balls, with a tilt of his head in my direction, said, "Might know he'd show up."

"Good to see you, too, Balls," I said.

Odell extended his hand and we shook. With a faint grin, he shook his head in response to Balls' greeting of me. People had a tendency to do a lot of head shaking around Balls.

Odell has finely chiseled features. His skin is the color of coffee tinted with a bit of cream. In profile, he's always reminded me of an ancient Roman coin. He has that sort of face—and a wry sense of humor. The silver nametag on his shirt reads O. Wright, and I heard him once tell a tourist that he is one of the original Wright Brothers. Then he excused himself from the bewildered visitor by explaining he had to go check on his crazy brother who was working on a contraption he thinks will fly.

I like Odell. He's an excellent lawman, too.

Balls said to Odell, "You come with us, and this dirty-neck ex-newspaper guy will buy you lunch, too."

"Appreciate it," Odell said, with a grin at me and then back to Balls. "But gonna go home. Supposed to be off this afternoon."

I noticed that Odell's shirt was a little wilted and he had a faint trace of silver whiskers as if he had missed shaving this morning. I knew what that meant. He had been on duty all night. Hmm. That was what Balls was doing here. Something was going on. Well, I'd probably get a bit of information from Balls later.

To me, Balls said, "You ready? You gotta go check with your sweetie downstairs before we can go?"

"I think we can go ahead and slip out, Balls."

Odell gave a lopsided hint of a smile and shook his head again.

Balls and I went out the back stairs because his Thunderbird was parked on Budleigh Street. As we got in his car, with me squeezing in careful not to bump the crowd of computer and radio equipment that took up a hefty portion of the front, he said, "Let's go eat at Darrell's . . . and you can tell me all about this imaginary psychopath that's stalking you."

"Well, I hope it is *imaginary*," I said.

Before we pulled away from the curb, Balls looked steadily at me and said, in a serious tone, "So do I."

Chapter Four

At Darrell's, we parked well around in the back, as far from other cars as Balls could possibly get. As usual, too, he backed into the parking space. Always ready to make a fast getaway—or go in pursuit.

We went in the restaurant and a cheery young woman with a great smile led us to a booth near the back on the left that Balls had pointed to. She put menus down and rattled off a couple or three of the lunch specials. I wasn't really listening. Balls had her repeat one of the items. Grilled pork chop with mashed potatoes, gravy, and green beans. He ordered that and sweet iced tea. I chose the fried oysters, one of their specialties.

"Since 1960, a favorite," Balls said.

"What?"

He pointed to a line on the menu. "A favorite since 1960," he said.

"Yes, one of the oldest continuously operated restaurants in the area," I said. "This one and Owens'. Owens' since 1946, I think it is, over in Nags Head. There may be others I just don't know about. Probably are. A few."

The waitress brought me water and Balls' sweet iced tea. He immediately started adding more sugar.

"Already sweet, isn't it?"

Balls ignored me. "Okay," he said, stirring the tea vigorously with his spoon, "give me the details again."

I went over the items, the messages, the occurrences—or whatever they were—in chronological order, starting with the book of short stories and how I didn't think that much of it, except as an interesting coincidence; then the cigarette butts, and how that began to get my attention. Of course the poor dead parakeet, with the same coloration as Janey, made me really sit up and take notice. Made me realize these weren't random events; they were linked. Someone was sending signals to me. But why? And what kind of signals?

Our food came just as I finished. Balls dived right in. I picked up my fork and looked across the table at Balls. "I'm not being paranoid, am I?"

"Afraid not," Balls said, hardly glancing up at me. He did some serious chewing and then plopped a pat of butter in with the gravy on the mashed potatoes, mixed it around a bit. He hadn't touched his green beans yet.

I ate one of the fried oysters. Delicious. Crisp breading and not overcooked.

Balls stopped eating and looked up at me. "When did you stop smoking Kools?"

"Oh, ten years at least. Just before I quit smoking cigarettes altogether."

He got something of a grin. "I remember you told me why you quit Kools. King-size Kools." He chuckled.

"Yes," I said. "Still sort of embarrassing. Back in the drinking days, too."

I had gone into the local drugstore to order cigarettes. I was trying my best to act completely sober and sophisticated, and probably failing miserably at both. Sauntering up to the young woman behind the counter, I'd said, "Give me a pack of Kool-size Kings." She had looked quizzically at me, and I realized what I had ordered didn't sound quite right. But I repeated it. "Kool-size Kings." She had started to say, "I'm sorry but I don't . . ." So I said, "Oh, just make it a pack of Kings." She had pushed a pack of Kools toward me. "This what you want?" I said, "Sure. They will do." Maybe I hadn't quit drinking that night, but I never ordered another pack of King-size Kools. I switched brands, just before stopping altogether with cigarettes.

And switching from alcohol to water wasn't far behind.

"Okay," I said to Balls, "let's talk about getting paranoid."

Balls stopped eating and looked me in the eyes. "You've really pissed somebody off." He made that humpf sound, sort of halfway between a grunt and a chuckle. "'Course you gotta tendency to do that anyway."

"That's not so. I'm a sweet, sensitive, and caring person, easy to get along with."

"Yeah, right," he said. He took another bite. I saw him eyeing my oysters. "They any good?"

"Sure. Try one . . ."

Before I had finished my sentence he had speared one from across the table and it disappeared promptly down his throat. "Yep. Not bad."

"How did you even taste it?"

He ignored me. "You smoked those Kools years ago. So if that's a message to you, has to be somebody known you a long time. Somebody you pissed off years back."

"That's what I figured."

"Think of anybody been holding a grudge against you for years?"

"No." I'd gone through in my mind some of the grievances I'm sure I'd caused back in those days. Even drinking, I wasn't belligerent or usually confrontational. Well, maybe a little. "But, my goodness, Balls, even if I had ruffled some feathers years ago, why all of a sudden these . . . these messages, or whatever they are?"

The waitress approached us. "Everything all right? Want anything else?"

"Maybe a couple more those hushpuppies be nice," Balls said.

"Sure thing," she said, and scurried toward the kitchen. She reappeared quickly with four hushpuppies, good and hot, on a small plate.

"Thank you," I said.

Balls took one, broke it in half, and slathered butter on both halves. They vanished. Despite the way he eats, Balls doesn't seem to gain excess weight. He's husky anyway, and strong. I've said before that he's one of those guys who was born tough and remained so; punching him in the midsection would be like slamming a fist into a solid burlap bag of wet sand. You'd just come back with sore knuckles and he wouldn't even make that humpf sound.

He frowned at the table, thinking. "And that parrot of yours . . ."

"Parakeet," I said.

"Whatever. The dead one looked just like yours?"

"Yes. Exact coloration." I shook my head. "But that's not all that unusual because lots of parakeets are yellow and green like that, or blue, and that's about it."

"You keep your house locked?"

"Well, not all the time. I've thought about that too. Be creepy if someone came and took a look at my parakeet . . ."

Balls waved a hand away dismissively. "Getting back to it, cigarettes like you used to smoke and a bird that looks like yours and a short story you've used in talks." He glanced up at me. "How long you used that short story?"

"Oh, golly, that goes back years. Heck, I first read it and talked about it in college."

"See what I mean?" he said. "Whoever this is has known you a long, long time."

"Yes, and like it's something that's been festering . . ."

He made a face as if he mulled over what I had just said. "Maybe festering, but not too seriously . . . so far anyway. Just bothersome things." He rubbed a big hand across his chin. "What I don't like, though, is seems like the messages get more serious each time. Playing games with you but getting more serious."

"Yes, that's what I've thought."

"Don't want this joker to get too serious." He picked up the last hushpuppy but didn't put it in his mouth immediately. He rolled it back and forth with his thumb and first two fingers. "On the surface, doesn't look like too much to get worried about. But it's deliberate and well thought out, and with the kind of work you do—writing about scumbags and crooks and killers—there could be somebody out there that's really taken a dislike to you."

I nodded. "I've thought about that too."

"Meantime, keep your eyes open. Watch for anyone hanging around, showing up where he wouldn't normally be. Keep me posted anything else appears."

"I will."

He eyed my plate. "You gonna eat that last oyster?"

Chapter Five

Late in the afternoon, Elly called me. "Why don't you come over a little early and have a truly hearty vegetable soup Mother's making and maybe a grilled cheese sandwich. We're eating light tonight, and then you and I can talk about Paris . . . Paris . . . oh, my gosh I can hardly believe it!"

"That sounds good, but I thought you might like to go to a movie—or do something else."

"Um-huh. I know about 'something else.'"

"Well, you know . . ."

"There'll be time, Mister." She spoke softly so her co-workers couldn't hear.

"Kind of you—and your mother. What, five, five-thirty?"

"Five-thirty or six would be fine. Give me time to get a little freshened up."

"You're always fresh."

"Um-huh. See you then."

I had plenty of time to take a shower and then actually practice major scales on the bass, using the bow. Then I played a couple of minor scales. Never felt as comfortable with the minor ones. I laid the bass down on its side in the living room. I have a stand for it but much of time it's sprawled on the living room floor and I have to step over the neck to go from one side of the room to the other.

Later as I drove south along the Bypass toward Manteo and Elly's, I kept an eye back and forth on the rear view mirror. I had in my sights a large dark Audi sedan. We didn't see too many of the Audis here at the beach, and maybe that's what made me notice. It was two or three cars back but kept up with me. From what little I could see, it appeared the side windows were tinted.

You really are getting paranoid, Harrison.

Nonetheless, I was aware of the Audi and noticed that when I changed lanes, it had a tendency to do the same. I figured maybe the driver was headed to one of the restaurants or maybe even on toward the Marc Basnight Bridge over Oregon Inlet to Hatteras. But the Audi was still back a few cars behind me when I swung to the right at Whalebone Junction, and it did the same.

The Audi was only one car behind me as I topped the Washington Baum Bridge over Roanoke Sound and started the descent toward Pirates Cove. I pushed the speed a tad over sixty. It kept pace. Then when I took the turn toward downtown Manteo, it was right behind me, figuratively pushing me like the driver wanted me to go faster.

Paranoid or not, I didn't like it.

However, at the third stoplight, as I kept straight, the Audi turned up Budleigh Street.

Okay, Harrison, quit looking for villains behind every stump.

I had virtually forgotten the Audi as I took the left off the highway onto the familiar street that runs close to Elly's house. Another left, a short couple of blocks and I pulled up in the drive, parking just to the left of her Nissan; her mother's older Pontiac was parked closer to the house.

The days were definitely getting shorter but there was still a great deal of light left. It had just gotten softer. Very mild, humidity not bad at all.

Some of Elly's son Martin's toys—a ray gun and two scratched up trucks, one with a wheel missing—were in the grassless sandy soil underneath the low, spreading branches of the huge life oak tree. Probably the tiny once-white small old-fashioned stove and a single miniature chair belonged to little Lauren, the next-door neighbor and playmate of Martin's.

As I approached the front porch, Elly pushed open the screen door and came out, followed as usual by Martin, who stood close beside her, eyeing me solemnly. He was not holding on to Elly's leg like he used to. Growing up a bit. Elly raised one hand and wiggled her fingers in greeting. Nice smile, too. She had changed into a pair of khaki shorts, soft pink golf shirt, and flip-flops. She had pinned her hair back, exposing her neck. I loved to kiss the back of her neck, especially just below where one or two wispy hairs had come loose.

I stepped up onto the porch and gave her a discreet peck on the cheek. She looked into my eyes and smiled warmly.

Putting a hand on Martin's shoulder, I said, "Hello, young man."

He nodded, still eyeing me.

As we went in, I was completely seduced by the hearty aroma of the homemade vegetable soup. "Oh, golly, that smells good, Mrs. Pedersen," I called.

From the kitchen, she said, "Welcome. Be ready in a minute."

Two table lamps were on in the living room. They were not really needed yet, but they gave a comforting glow to the room that I liked. Today's half-finished crossword puzzle was folded on the end table nearest me.

Elly saw me looking at the puzzle. "I've had a bit of trouble with this one."

"They get harder as the week goes by, don't they?"

"Yes, but . . . oh, well."

She worked them every day and she was good at it. Rarely had any real trouble.

Mrs. Pedersen came into the living room. She had a dishtowel she shifted from one hand to the next, drying her hands. She's taller than Elly and has an erect bearing and short gray hair that she brushes back rather severely. Her hair looks like metal. She's imposing until she smiles warmly and her whole countenance lightens. Looking at the mother and daughter together you know that Elly must have taken after her father, a native of Minnesota, who came to the area in the Coast Guard. He was lost at sea in a violent storm a good fifteen years ago.

"Supper's ready," Mrs. Pedersen said, adding, "Such as 'tis."

"Smells wonderful," I said, and it did. We went into the small dining room with its round table. Three large filled and steaming soup bowls were set out, and a smaller one was set for Martin. A plate of homemade biscuits graced the center of the table and a shallow bowl of saltine crackers were close to Martin's place. Also on the table were a butter dish and a jar of locally produced honey. The soup was tomato colored with plenty of vegetables and chunks of beef.

We sat and I breathed in the aroma of the soup.

The soup was as tasty as it smelled, and plenty hearty also. I kept eyeing the biscuits and the butter and honey as I ate.

"Would you like some more soup?" Mrs. Pedersen said. "There's plenty more." She took a half-spoonful of her own soup. "I think it's always better the second day. So I make plenty."

"I'm fine," I said.

"I think he's got his mouth set on some of those biscuits," Elly said.

". . . and honey and butter," I added. Mrs. Pedersen made biscuits almost every day. No canned Pillsbury for her. In a separate small plate, I whipped together honey and butter, opened one of the still-warm biscuits, slathered it with the mixture and went at it.

"I like to see a man eat," Mrs. Pedersen said, turning that smile at me.

"I'm eating, too," Martin said, crushing more saltines into his thickening soup.

"Yes, you are," Elly said. "That's good. You're doing

fine."

All but Martin declined a slice of apple pie. He got a small scoop of vanilla ice cream on his. The ice cream began melting into rivulets as it touched the warm pie.

Shortly, after thanking Mrs. Pedersen for the meal, Martin and I went into the living room while Elly helped her mother. Martin, with an eye toward me, retrieved a drawing from a folder on the coffee table. He handed it to me.

"Oh, this is good, Martin. You're getting better all the time." And he was. He had graduated from the mostly stick figures he used to draw to fleshed-out people. The scene he had drawn was of three people—a man, woman and smaller boy, backs to the viewer as they looked out at what had to be the ocean. "You really are," I said, studying the drawing. Heck, he was barely six and this showed real talent. "I believe you're going to be a famous artist," I said.

For the first time that evening, he gave me a shy smile.

When Elly came into the living room, I said, "Martin is really getting good at his artwork."

"Yes, he is," Elly said, and touched Martin lightly on the head. "He really is. I know I'm biased but he's definitely got talent, I think."

"No question about it," I said.

Martin sprawled out on the living room floor, art folder at his elbow, and began serious and solemn work again.

Elly and I went out on the front porch and sat together in the bench swing that was suspended from the ceiling by a set of chains. We rocked gently as we sat. She put her hand on top of mine and looked at me and smiled and neither of us said anything.

After a moment, she said, "Okay, let's dream about Paris . . . and what I must pack. Getting closer, you know."

"Yes, just a couple more weeks," I said.

"Eleven days," she said. "I've been checking the weather, two or three times a day. It seems like it's all over the place."

"Layers."

"What?"

"Take layers. So you can add to or take off."

We had been to Paris a year and a half earlier with Balls and his wife, Lorraine. Un-huh, as Elly said, as chaperones. This time we were going alone and had rented a little apartment I knew about on rue des Grands Degres in the fifth arrondissement, edge of the Latin Quarter and a couple of blocks from Shakespeare and Company, and two more blocks to my favorite, the Abbey Bookshop.

Although Elly's hometown of Manteo is a place where the locals all know each other, she agreed to throw caution— and maybe her reputation—to the wind and just the two of us take off for a vacation together. After all, we had become known increasingly as a couple. Let the tongues wag, she said. Give folks something to gossip about.

I said, "It'll be early September, so the weather should be pleasant and mild most of the time."

"What about dressy?"

"Not really needed. You always look nice."

"Yeah, sure."

Then she looked at me as I stared off into the distance. I turned my head enough to catch her expression from the corner of my eye. "What is it?"

"What is it you're mulling over in your mind?" she asked.

"Oh, nothing. Nothing really, just sort of enjoying the evening."

"I know you better than that," she said.

I shrugged. "Nothing, really." Actually, I thought about the messages that had been left—the parakeet, the cigarette butts, the short story. But I wasn't ready to get into any of that with Elly.

Not yet.

Chapter Six

That night driving home, I kept an eye out for the dark Audi sedan. Nowhere in sight, and I chided myself for letting my imagination run away with me.

The next day, I drove down to Manteo to pick up a book by Amor Towles that Jamie had ordered for me. After visiting with her for ten or fifteen minutes, part of that time talking about the Towles book I had bought, *Rules of Civility*, she mentioned she liked it better than his *Gentleman in Moscow*; thought it was faster paced. *Gentleman*, though, was so very well done, I'd said, especially the ending.

A customer came to the counter and I waved a goodbye and went out into the sunshine and warmth, crossed Sir Walter Raleigh Street, and approached my car when I noticed a piece of paper had been affixed under my windshield wiper. I figured it was an advertisement of some kind.

But it wasn't.

It was a newspaper clipping. I unfolded it. The headline chilled me. "Young Child Witnesses Mother Being Slain; Killer Sought." It was a story from the Raleigh *News & Observer*, published five days ago. The son in the story, who was a year younger than Martin, had seen his mother being stabbed to death. They had lived about an hour from Raleigh toward Rocky Mount, only about three hours from the Outer Banks. She was a single mother. Police said the son was too young to give an accurate description of the killer, except that he was male and tall and wore a coat. Investigators said they had established no motive, nor did they have a suspect. Police questioned her boyfriend, but he was at a conference in Washington when the woman was murdered.

I remained standing beside my car, the clipping in my hand. I glanced around as if I expected I might see the person who had placed the article on my windshield. Of course, I didn't.

Opening the car door, I slipped inside, turned the switch to lower the windows. Light perspiration beaded on my forehead and I could feel dampness between my shoulder blades. I sat there quietly, thinking, staring straight ahead. Did an acquaintance come across this news story and think it might be something I would want to write about, knew my car, and stuck it on the windshield in a helpful manner?

Maybe possible.

But I didn't think so.

No, I thought it was another message to me, and a message that caused me deep concern, a gnawing anger. It involved a single mother—like Elly—and a young son—like Martin.

Were they now in the crosshairs of this son of a bitch who was doing this?

As I sat there, I was barely conscious of an automobile that crept slowly past me. It was an Audi, a dark one, tinted windows. I turned quickly, as it passed. It was gone before I could check the license tag. Judging from the color of the tags, I got the impression it was an out-of-state license. But my impression was so fleeting, I couldn't be sure.

I started to give—what? pursuit?—then realized how useless that would be. A tad foolish.

But it was time, I knew, that I had to talk to Elly about my suspicions, that someone was sending me messages. And now, damnit, the person might also be sending messages to or about Elly.

First, though, I wanted to mull all of this over in my mind, and talk again with Balls. I drove home a bit slower than usual, keeping an eye out for other cars.

When I got to my little blue house, I went up the outside

stairs and unlocked the door. I had started locking it. Previously I went most of the day without bothering to lock the doors. It wasn't a pleasant feeling, knowing now that I judiciously locked up every time I left the house for only an hour or so.

I spoke to Janey and put my hand inside her cage to touch her. I was happy to see her alive and well. Stepping over the neck of the bass fiddle, I went to the phone. No messages. I took a seat and then punched in Balls' cell phone.

He answered on the first ring. "Yeah? Whadda you want?"

"This may seem sort of out in left field, Balls, but on my windshield this morning, someone had stuck a news clip about . . ." And I went into detail about the story. I even mentioned my suspicions about an Audi sedan that seemed to keep showing up.

He was silent and let me go on at quite a length. When I finished, I waited a moment. Then he said, and he said it seriously and without the usual Balls gruffness, "When are you and Elly going to Paris."

That caught me off guard. Then it made sense. "Next week," I said.

"I'd feel better if you were leaving today."

"Yes, me too," I said.

"I'll be down there tomorrow," he said. "With Odell. Hell, ought a get me an apartment down there, way I keep going back and forth."

"See you then?"

"Maybe. Got other things to do besides babysit you."

"Yes, I know," I said. My voice sounded dispirited.

He got serious again. "Meantime, keep your sweetie—keep Elly—safe."

"Yeah," I said, sounding almost like Balls, with a "yeah" instead of a "yes."

We hung up, and I sat there in the rickety chair a moment longer. I should get a better chair. Then the phone rang. I figured it was Balls calling back.

But it wasn't.

A voice, sounding distorted and disguised, said, "This is just the beginning." Then the phone went dead. The caller ID was a number I didn't recognize.

Immediately, I called Balls. I told him about the call.

"As I've said, you've really pissed somebody off."

"Think it's just somebody playing games?"

He was quiet for a moment. "Naw, I don't. Afraid it might be serious. Too well thought out, planned. Not just a game."

Again sounding like Balls, I said, "Naw, I don't think it's just a game either."

"You still got that little pea-shooter?" He referred to a .32 caliber revolver he knew I had tucked away somewhere.

"Yes . . ." I said. My voice trailed off.

"Keep it with you."

"You think that might be a bit . . . a bit extreme?"

"I hope so," he said.

After we hung up for the second time. I stared at the phone and dared it to ring. It didn't.

I knew I needed to talk with Elly. Without alarming her too much, I wanted to have her be alert, be safe. How I crafted what I had to say to her, however, would be the hard part. Just enough, but not too much. Crap, that was always difficult to do.

Checking the time, I called her at work. Becky answered the phone and then summoned Elly in the singsong tease of a voice. "Someone special," she said.

Elly picked up. "This someone special?"

"Absolutely," I said. "At least I hope so."

Maybe there was something in my voice. "What's up?" she said, her tone more subdued.

"Well, I thought you might have time for a cup of coffee when you get off . . . and before you go home."

"I'll say again, Harrison. What's up? Remember, I know you well."

"Okay," I said. "Something I need to talk with you about. Nothing too serious. Just need to run a couple of things by you."

"Are we still going to Paris?"

"Oh, yes, certainly."

She was silent a beat or two. "I can leave fifteen minutes or so early, if that's better."

"Yes," I said. "Upstairs at the coffee shop?" I referred to the coffee and pastry café across Sir Walter Raleigh Street from the courthouse.

"See you then," she said, that serious tone even more pronounced in her voice.

With plenty of time left in the afternoon to get to the coffee shop in time, I retrieved my .32 revolver from the bedside table, where I kept it oiled, loaded, and wrapped inside a thick old sock. I used to have a flimsy dishtowel around the gun. But in a sock, it could also be swung as a club. I laid it, sock and all, on the kitchen counter. I spoke to Janey again and decided to give her a fresh sprig of millet. A little treat she loved. I knew I was being more solicitous of her than usual perhaps. I was just glad she was alive and chirpy.

When I put the millet in her cage, secured with a wooden clothes pen, she did her head-bobbing little dance and said, "Shit," but she said it happily. It was one of the only two words she mimicked. The other one was "bitch," and she said that one perfectly, too. Female parakeets are not supposed to talk at all. She had obviously picked up these two words from me as I had spent hours trying to perfect a section of Mozart's "Requiem" on the bass that required crossing over the strings with the bow without miscuing and making it sound like a cat in distress. I was convinced that Mozart hated bass players. I had cussed a lot as I practiced. And Janey had listened to me.

I locked up the house as I left for Manteo. With the revolver held close against my thigh, I went down the stairs and got in the Subaru, securing the gun under the front seat. The weather was well into the eighties and the humidity had risen. Typical late August day here on the barrier islands. A thin smear of clouds kept the sun looking almost opaque, like through beveled glass. Traffic was heavy on the Bypass. Late afternoon tourists, having spent time probably out on the beach, meandered along the road as if they couldn't decide exactly where they wanted to go next. I did my best not to be frustrated. After all, I had plenty of time and I needed to fashion in my mind exactly what I would tell Elly. Rather, how much I would tell her.

I found a place to park in the little alley just on the south side of the coffee shop, and I walked up the back stairs. Inside I ordered a single espresso, and took it to one of the little tables on the narrow front porch.

No sooner had I seated than I saw Elly leaving the front of the courthouse and cutting diagonally across the street.

Those two little worry creases were between her eyebrows.

And I pondered again, exactly how much concern to express to her.

Chapter Seven

She came up the side steps in front. I stood as she approached. She had a smile, but there was a touch of wariness in it. I reached around the table and moved her chair out. Before I sat I asked if she'd like a coffee. She declined, said she didn't care for anything. Tilting her head slightly to one side, she had an unspoken question in her demeanor.

Then it ceased to be unspoken. "All right, Harrison," she said, "will you tell me what's up?" She was one of the few people who used my full first name. Most of my acquaintances referred to me as Weav.

"Well, it's probably nothing, but there may be somebody out there who is playing games on me."

"Games?"

"You know, leaving little clues that he is trying to play games with my imagination."

"What sort of clues?"

I wasn't going to get by with too much vagueness, not with Elly. "Well, leaving cigarette butts of a brand I used to smoke where I'd find them. End of my driveway."

She raised one eyebrow as if to say, "Go on . . ."

"And I guess the worst thing was a dead parakeet, leaving a dead parakeet that looked a lot like Janey, on my stairs."

Her face fully registered her feelings. "That's horrible, Harrison. What's this all about?"

"Well, only reason I'm bringing it up is because . . . well, because I want you to keep an eye open in case you notice anything sort of out of the usual. I mean, something that strikes you as not as it should be . . ."

She looked straight at me, her expression one of stern concern. "There's more to this than what you're saying, Harrison. I know you well enough to know that." She breathed out, maybe a touch of exasperation showing. "Give me credit, please."

"I think it's just someone who knows me, or someone I've offended in some way, who's playing games with me, wants to, you know, bug me. That's what I think. A game." I was lying of course, and she knew that too. I wouldn't have asked her to meet me to tell me this if I thought it was no more than someone playing tricks on me.

She eyed my coffee. "Maybe I will have an espresso. Single one, two sugars."

"Be right back with it," I said, and tried a smile, which she didn't return. I got up and went inside. When I brought her coffee and a paper napkin, she eyed me as I took my seat.

"Thank you," she said. She got the tiniest hint of a wry smile. "Okay, what does Agent Twiddy say about this?"

"Balls?"

"Yes. What does he say? I *know* you've talked with him."

I took the last sip of my now-cold espresso. "He thinks it may be more than a game, a little more serious."

Elly nodded. "I'm sure he does," she said. "And so do I. So do you. You wouldn't have called this"—she gave a half chuckle—"this meeting unless you thought so too."

I conceded. "That's true, but I didn't want to alarm you, make you worry."

Again that wry smile of hers. "When did you ever *not* alarm me, worry me?" She stirred her coffee vigorously with the tiny silver spoon, took a sip, touched the napkin to her lips. I always admired the perfect bow at the top of her upper lip. "Quit staring," she said. Then, "Tell me the rest of it."

"He thinks it could be some . . . some nut case from my past who really resents me for some reason. He wants me to keep alert, let him know if there's anything else, and he wanted me to tell you to be careful and let me know if you notice anything, you know, unusual."

"Like what? An axe-wielding, wild-eyed killer lurking about?" She tried to put humor in her statement, but she was having a hard time of it. She looked down at her half-finished espresso. "I didn't really want this. I don't know why I asked you to get it for me. But thank you."

I nodded, thinking. I was almost on the verge of telling her about the news article that was on my windshield, and then the telephone call.

Studying me, she kept silent. I could feel her eyes on me. After a half a minute, she said, "Is there something else you want to tell me?"

I mulled it over. "No, not now." Once again, I tried a smile. "But I will certainly keep you posted."

"That sounds businesslike enough to mean nothing at all."

We saw Becky leaving the courthouse. Elly glanced at her wristwatch. "She's not exactly putting in overtime."

"Well, it is five."

"Right on the button," Elly said.

It was then that I saw the Audi drive by slowly. Elly saw my body tense as I twisted to try to get a better look at the sedan. Still too far away to read the license tag but it was not a North Carolina tag. Maybe a rental?

"What is it?" Elly said. "That car?"

"Yes, I keep seeing it . . . too often," I said.

"Your *friend*, you think?"

I shrugged. "Don't want to start imagining things."

"Knowing you, I doubt if you are—imaging things."

The Audi continued down Sir Walter Raleigh Street toward the highway. I settled back in my chair.

Elly glanced again at her watch. "I ought to head on home," she said.

"Understand." I knew I sounded distracted.

"You okay?"

"Oh, fine. Sure."

"Thank you again for the espresso." She looked at her half full little cup.

"I'll finish it," I said.

"Waste not . . . et cetera," she said, and started getting up.

I rose. "I'll be heading back in a minute."

That half-smile again. "Keep me posted, as they say in the business world."

"I will." I leaned forward and gave her a kiss on the cheek. "See you tomorrow night? A real date? Movie maybe? . . . Or something."

A true smile this time. "Or something . . ."

I watched her leave, and I sat back down and took the last of her espresso. Well, I hadn't told her everything, not by a long shot, but she knew me well enough to know that there *was* more and that it would come out sooner or later.

In just a few minutes, I picked up the two cups and carried them inside.

The young woman behind the counter said, "Oh, thank you very much. I could have got those."

I eyed the pastries behind the glass and was tempted, but knew I needed to get home and eat a regular meal. The espresso and a half had me a bit wired. At the same time, I felt a bit drained. I'm sure that was from telling Elly part of the story, worrying about the rest, and wondering what in the hell was going on. It was no game. I couldn't believe that it was.

Someone out there was planning carefully, deliberately, diabolically.

I hate the overuse of the word "psychopath." And I didn't want to use it. But at the same time, this was not normal behavior. Even though each happening, each message could be explained away, taken together . . .

And there was no way to dismiss the phone call . . . that it was just beginning.

Chapter Eight

Each day I searched the Internet news stories trying to track down any further information about the slaying of the young mother witnessed by her son. Saturday morning there was a follow-up story and a recap of what the police investigators knew at this point—which was damn little. But it did give more detail as to where the murder had occurred.

The mother and young son had prepared to enter their house, which was separated from their nearest neighbor by a vacant lot, when the assailant apparently rushed up to the two of them and stabbed her twice in the back and once in the chest. The killer then ran away, leaving the unharmed boy there with his dying mother, until a passing neighbor happened to see them. Detective J. W. Doles said there was no motive they could determine; robbery was not attempted; he said it was almost like a random killing. "It was vicious, quick, and deadly," he said. "The victim was pronounced dead at the scene. The assailant knew where to strike to kill."

It would really be a stretch, I knew, for the person leaving me messages to be the same one who had killed the mother. But why leave me the clipping? Just to tease me, show me he was out there? Unless it was left by someone in the community who knew I was a crime writer. I continued to doubt this.

I tried, more or less successfully, to put that slaying out of my mind. But there was something so terrible, unspeakable about killing a mother in front of her child . . .

I got busy with some writing that Rose, my editor, was looking for. It went so-so; I was having a difficult time getting into it. It was a short piece and I was about finished with it, and I promised her I'd deliver it before we went to Paris, and that time was coming up fast. And I'd be busy almost every day. Date with Elly tonight, and I was looking forward to that; then flying lesson tomorrow morning early with Samantha Inez Davis, or Sam, as she was known; then the final gig of the season on Wednesday at Scarborough Faire up in Duck with Jim Watson's jazz combo. Thursday morning we'd leave for Paris.

Oh, yes, pack, too. But that wouldn't take me long. Couple of hours, tops. And I'd have to take Janey over to neighbor Misty, who had agreed to be her caretaker during the ten days we would be gone.

Later that afternoon I took a shower. Then I remembered I hadn't eaten lunch, so snacked a bit on cheese, crackers, and some nice local scuppernong grapes that had just come in at Food Lion. During the summer I had practically lived on Bing cherries. I wished they were available longer in the summer.

For maybe one of the last times for the season, I put on khaki shorts and sockless boat shoes, a blue cotton golf shirt. No shorts to Paris in September, or maybe any other month as far as I knew.

We had agreed I'd pick Elly up at six-thirty. We would eat shrimp at Sugar Creek, watch the sunset over Shallow Bag Bay.

As I topped the bridge driving over to Elly's late that afternoon, I looked at how the distant trees silhouetted black against the lowering sun.

I was feeling good and looking forward to being with her tonight. After dinner, I hoped for an interlude at my house.

Elly didn't come out on her front porch as she often did when I drove up. But she was there at the screen door, ushering me in with a smile and peck on the cheek. Martin and Mrs. Pedersen were in the living room. The television was on, but turned low. I think it was an old movie. Maybe something on Netflix. Martin was busy drawing. He sat cross-legged at the coffee table, his big art pad and colored pencils in front of him.

"I've been packing," Elly said.

"More like she's been fretting *about* packing and what to take," Mrs. Pedersen said with a laugh, and turned back to the TV screen.

With a smile and a dismissive toss of her head, Elly said, "Ready to go?"

Before we left, I took a look at Martin's latest drawings, and I complimented him, sincerely.

I opened the passenger door for Elly, and she said, "Thank you, sir. Always the Southern gentleman."

"Sign of early toilet training," I said. "Gets ingrained."

Although we occasionally went to Lone Cedar or Tale of the Whale, and they were good, I guess our favorite along the causeway was Sugar Creek. I loved their lightly breaded fried shrimp. Owner Ervin Bateman was usually there in the evenings to greet us.

We were seated at a table looking toward Shallow Bag Bay. The water glistened in the fading light and a few birds worked the surface, hoping for a small fish or two.

Elly arranged her napkin and her flatware. She looked up at me. "Any more messages—or whatever they are—from that person out there?"

"All quiet on the western front," I said.

"A movie? Or World War I novel? I know it is. German writer."

"Yes, good for you," I said.

"Well, maybe whoever it is, has had his fun . . . and that's the end of it."

"Yes, maybe so," I said, not believing it for a minute.

Elly ordered the grilled flounder, and, yes, the shrimp for me. Baked potato and coleslaw. The works for the baked potato, butter and sour cream, salt and pepper, bacon bits and a touch of cheese. The potato was steaming hot and the butter and sour cream soaked right in. Cornbread, too, that had a teasing sweetness to it.

"If we don't take in a movie, we could swing by my house for coffee or something," I said.

She raised an eyebrow, tilted her head. ". . . or something, huh?"

"Well, you know . . ." I said.

She gave a short little laugh. "Yes, I know," she said. Then she faked that mischievous smile. "You know we'll have all that time in Paris, without a chaperone."

"Yes, but we'll be tired and all after the overnight flight, and . . ."

"You're terrible," she said, and laughed. "Okay, hurry up and eat."

With mock urgency, I shoveled in two bites of potato and a shrimp and chewed away. Raising my hand to the waitress who was not there, I said, "Check! Check!"

We both laughed and slowed down in our eating.

But we didn't exactly linger over the meal.

Driving up to my house, we were quiet, but she touched my knee twice. It felt good, promising.

I thought about retrieving my revolver from under the front seat and taking it in with me, but I knew that would bring questions and concerns from Elly, maybe even dispel the aura that had built up between us. Well, I'd bring it in tonight when I came back to the house.

Unlocking the door to the house, I held the door open for her and we went in and Janey chirped and then said, "Bitch."

"Same to you, Janey," Elly said.

We embraced and kissed, and then we headed for the bedroom. You'd think there was an urgency that had never been met. Neither one of us had on much clothing, and it didn't take long. But when we were undressed and facing each other, I held both of her hands in mind and looked her up and down. "Lovely," I said. "Absolutely lovely. I love the mysterious little triangle. The hidden road to exquisite pleasure."

"A writer, yes," she said. She raised that eyebrow again, looking at me. "Not bad yourself, sir . . ." She chuckled. "But a bit menacing."

"Come here," I said, and we tumbled onto the bed.

Later, we got dressed, and a little more slowly.

"Paris will be fun, won't it?" she said when we went into the living room and prepared to leave.

"It's always wonderful," I said.

"This is what, your tenth trip there?"

"Something like that," I said.

I left two lamps on in the living room and one on over my work area in what passed as a dinette area. Locking the door, I told Janey I'd see her later. She sat there with her feathers sort of fluffed up. She was silent, eyeing me.

"She doesn't like me," Elly said as we started down the stairs.

"Jealous," I said.

Since the Subaru was parked close to the door of the utility room, we went around to the rear of the car for me to open the passenger door for Elly.

Then I saw the cigarette butts.

I stopped and so did Elly. We both looked down at them. A couple of feet from the rear of the car. Just under the edge of the carport. Two fresh half-smoked cigarettes. Without picking them up, I knew they were Kools. Had to be. They had not been there earlier. While we had been inside making love, someone . . .

I didn't want to think about it.

Using a tissue from a pack in the door of the Subaru, I picked up the butts, wrapped them carefully and laid them on the backseat.

"DNA or something?" Elly said. Her voice was strained and tense. It was almost a whisper.

I shook my head. "I wish," I said. "But not like TV . . . trying to get something done would be like . . . well, impossible."

We got in the car and I started the engine and backed out slowly. I kept looking around as we left the cul-de-sac and headed up toward the Bypass.

We were silent. I was aware we both watched the traffic, front and back. She kept leaning forward to peer in the side mirror, see behind her.

A mile or so down the Bypass, Elly spoke for the first time since we had started. "Harrison," she said, "I'm scared."

I nodded. "At least we'll be going to Paris in a few days."

"Yes," she said. "At least we'll be going to Paris."

Chapter Nine

After the subdued trip taking Elly home, and a kiss good-night inside her living room, where there was only the one table lamp still on, I stepped out on her front porch and waved. I know she waved back but I couldn't see her. I heard her lock the front door. One of the few times it was probably ever locked.

Driving back home, I was aware of virtually every vehicle in sight. Hell of an emotional and mental state to be in. I didn't like it.

I pulled in under my carport and retrieved my revolver, holding the thick sock by the top opening so it swung like a hefty club. It felt good. I locked my car. Jeez, lot of locking going on; quite unusual; a ritual that I hoped would not be the new norm.

Upstairs, I checked the time. Shortly after ten-thirty. Too late to call Balls, but I did anyway. His cell phone went straight to voice mail. "Apologize about the late call, but I found two more cigarette butts in my carport tonight. Someone was here while Elly and I were inside. Haven't seen anyone."

I hung up and before I got out of the chair, Balls called back. "When you getting out of Dodge?"

"We leave Thursday."

"Wish you were leaving tonight." In the very next phase, he couldn't help but be Balls. "Maybe then I could get some sleep."

"What do you think, Balls? I mean, really. Seriously."

"As I've told you, Sport, I think you need to be ready for

the worst. Possible just some joker trying to bug you . . . naw, I don't believe that. It's too persistent. Too well thought out. I been doing some rereading about psychopaths, and we had some of this up at Quantico in the FBI training, some of 'em—these nut jobs—get really hung up on somebody they think has slighted them or done something that sort of grows in their minds. Or somebody has reached success they think should be theirs and they resent it, hate the person . . . and this hate or obsession grows and grows until—bang!"

This was one of the longest speeches I'd heard Balls make. He'd obviously given thought to this. Sadly, he voiced thoughts that I'd barely permitted myself to think. "Yes . . ." I said and let my voice trail off. I didn't know what else to say.

Balls was ready to end it. "Lock up good. Keep that pea-shooter handy. Check with me if there's anything else. Hell, I know you will. Now, how 'bout letting me get some sleep?"

I went into my bedroom and took the revolver out of its sock and laid it naked on the bedside table. Opening the drawer to my table, I folded the thick sock and stuck it in a far corner. Before closing the drawer, I looked at the typed first paragraph of Hemingway's *A Farewell to Arms* that I keep in the drawer. I've used that first paragraph in several talks I've given on writing. The paragraph serves two purposes for me.

First, when I feel the need to be inspired, I reread that paragraph for the umpteenth time and marvel at it. The paragraph is a fine example of what narrative *can* be. It's got mood-setting, almost poetic rhythm, symbolism—it's got it all. Just the first few words: *In the late summer of that year* . . . Not the spring, not even midsummer, but late summer, when things are beginning to wilt and die. And then *of that year* . . . Wow, you know there's bound to be something special about *that year*.

The second purpose is professional.

When I start to feel uppity, like maybe I'm learning how to write, then I read that paragraph and it puts me in my place. No way, ever, will I attain that level.

I closed the drawer. Time to try to sleep. I wasn't sure sleep would come all that easy for me. And I had an early morning flying lesson with Sam tomorrow. I set the alarm, with plenty of time for coffee and driving to the Manteo airport.

Actually I slept better than I thought I would, and I was wide awake and drinking coffee by shortly after six Sunday morning. As I prepared to leave, I put my revolver back in its sock, and grabbed my sunglasses. Traffic was light and the morning looked great for flying. Light breeze from the southwest, clear skies. I was at the airport a little early, but Sam was already inside talking with Jesse, one of her young pilots.

She wore knee-length shorts, sneakers, and one of her company-logo golf shirts. Sam is about five-seven, trim, reddish hair that she keeps rather short. High cheekbones and has the looks that could serve her as a professional model. She was a little paler than she was earlier in the summer— before she was shot. Yes, I was flying with her as we chased down some human traffickers who began shooting at us, hitting the Cessna. One of the bullets had torn into the flesh at her waist. She lost a lot of blood but nothing vital was hit, and we—mostly me—managed to land the plane back safely . . . but barely. She spent several days in the hospital and now was back flying just a few weeks later.

"Okay, Fly Boy, ready to go?" She chuckled. "Better practice some touch-and-go landings. Get you more proficient."

We walked side by side out on the tarmac to the Cessna 172 that was parked off to the right. With the sunlight sparkling off the fresh blue and yellow paint, the plane looked right regal.

"Preflight check?" I said.

"Absolutely. Got to be ingrained in you. Doesn't matter that Jesse had it gassed and all, ready to go, you never get set to fly until you've done the full preflight routine, skipping nothing, and doing it in the same sequence each time so you know you got it right."

It takes several minutes, but it's a few minutes that could save you from a whole lot of hurting.

Sam watched me carefully and closely. Made sure I didn't skip anything, from checking the fuel, to the air stall horn, to the tire pressure, to the oil level, and finishing by running my hands over the prop, feeling for any nicks.

"Okay, good," she said. "Let's take a spin."

During the lesson, Sam had me practice sharp banks around the Bodie Lighthouse without losing altitude, and a few stop-and-go landings. The session gave me back some of my sense of equilibrium. If I could control a plane thousands of feet above the ground, surely I could handle some loser from past who wanted to play head games.

At the end of the lesson, I taxied the Cessna over near the office. We unbuckled and got out as Jesse came up. In a few minutes, he had a sightseeing flight for three passengers. Walking back to the office, I permitted myself a bit of a swagger, still probably grinning. It was fun and exhilarating, and I felt good about the lesson.

"We'll set a time for when you get back from Paris," Sam said when we stepped inside. She took out her calendar from her flight bag.

I pointed to a date in late September. "Just pencil in here," I said, "and I'll confirm with you when we—when I— get back."

Sam didn't miss the "we." I caught the look she gave me. I guess most folks around here know that Elly and I are, well, going steady as they used to say.

And thinking of Elly, I really wanted to stop by to see

her. But I knew she was busy packing and repacking and she wanted to spend as much uninterrupted time with Martin as she could in the next three days. The ten days going and coming from Paris would be the longest stretch of time she had ever been away from him.

So I drove away from the airport—and the vicinity of Elly's house—and headed back home. With the excitement of the flying lesson and concentrating on that, I realized I had given virtually no thought to that sonofabitch that was out there somewhere.

That is, I gave no thought to him until I was out on the main road and caught myself studying every car that approached me—front and rear.

Nothing suspicious met me coming or going. I got home and pulled in under the carport. I retrieved the revolver from under the front seat. As I got out, I automatically looked on the ground for more cigarette butts. There were none.

I went up the stairs and unlocked the door. Janey gave her welcoming chirps. I spoke to her and put my hand inside her cage, let her perch on my finger and nibble at a knuckle. I used to let her out of the cage more, but she was more of a homebody and liked her cage, liked being inside her little house. I've had a couple of male parakeets that liked to explore the houses where I had lived. Not Janey; she seems perfectly content inside the cage.

Almost lunchtime. Early, but might as well. Then maybe I'd begin my preliminary packing. I could do it in one medium-size suitcase and my laptop. Elly had already said she would take a large suitcase and a smaller one.

Later that afternoon, after I'd done some truly pre-preliminary packing, I shoved the suitcase over to the far side of the bed and stretched out a bit. After all, weren't Sunday afternoons made for napping?

I must have fallen sound asleep because when the phone on the bedside table rang, it jarred me awake, and without rousing myself even on an elbow, I reached over, fumbled with the handset, and mumbled a hello.

A pause and then that disguised voice said, "Wouldn't you like to smoke another Kool cigarette . . . like you used to?"

I was wide wake. "Listen, you son of a bitch . . ."

But with a chuckle at his end, the phone went dead.

I sat on the edge of the bed and rubbed my face. No question about it. This guy was someone from my past.

But who?

What had I done to warrant this from him?

And as Balls said, it wasn't near the end. Balls had said it usually ended with a "Bang."

As in, "You're dead."

Chapter Ten

The remainder of Sunday was pretty much ruined for me. I thought about calling Balls and confirming what I think both of us knew, that this was definitely someone from my past who had become obsessed with me and wanted to torment me, and maybe—according to Balls—to do me harm when he was through with his sick preliminaries, his psychotic foreplay. The possibility of harm to me, and even Elly and, my God, even to Martin, wasn't far from the forefront of my mind.

But if the newspaper clipping was a warning, it was only Elly who was in danger. The woman in the clipping was the target, her traumatized son only a witness. A horrible thing for him, something that will haunt him all of his life. But at least his life was spared.

I decided to wait until Monday to go over this latest with Balls, maybe bring Chief Deputy Odell Wright in on it too. Yes, that would be a good idea.

Needed to call Elly. Not go over this phone call with her, but just chat. However, I ought to calm down first, get my voice sounding moderately upbeat. Otherwise Elly would read right through me.

Before the night was through, the phone rang again. I double-checked caller ID before I answered. Okay, it was Jim Watson, and I welcomed the call.

"Good news for us on this Wednesday gig," he said. "Betsy Robinson is going to be our girl singer."

I hadn't heard the term "girl singer" in years. But I was delighted. Loved the way she could belt out a song with her really great voice; excellent sense of rhythm, which some "girl singers" of the past had lacked.

Jim, an excellent mid-range jazz trumpet player, went on to say, "Since this is our last gig at Scarborough Faire for the season, the management agreed to let me add Betsy."

We were to play at the end of the wooden walkway near Island Bookstore from one in the afternoon until three. It was always a fun job and we'd played several Wednesday afternoons there this summer. No more gigs until close to Thanksgiving, and that suited me fine. I knew I needed to spend more time on my writing—heck, making a living—and I was also working on a book of short stories, most of which had nothing at all to do with murder and mayhem, that an editor friend of Rose's had expressed enthusiastic interest in.

After talking about music with Jim, I felt comfortable calling Elly, and we chatted for quite a while. She went over with me a list of some of the outfits she was taking to Paris. Plenty of clothes that could be layered, leggings, skirts to go over them, a couple of semi-dressy tops, just in case. I probably wasn't much help, but I listened and made appropriate comments.

I didn't mention the disturbing call I had received. Well, maybe tomorrow, or at some point.

Before locking up that night, I cut back the lights in the living room and in the kitchen and sat outside in the dark. I sat a long time, just hoping that son of a bitch would show up.

I held my .32 revolver on my lap.

The night was quiet, the stars out by the millions. The breeze was still light and had shifted more from the east. The air smelled of the salt from the ocean, at least it seemed to me that it did. I took deep breaths.

The only activity in my cul-de-sac came about nine-thirty when my neighbor Misty came home and her inside house lights went on. Close to ten, I went inside, locked and secured the sliding glass door to the deck, rechecked the locked door at the kitchen, and got ready for bed, with my

CALLING CARDS OF DEATH

revolver handy on the bedside table.

I slept soundly all night and didn't wake until shortly after six. Seems I'd become more and more of an early riser. A few years earlier, when my wife Keely was still alive and we both played with musical groups more frequently—me on bass, Keely as a wonderful jazz singer—we slept late in the mornings.

I showered, drank coffee, and ate a bit, then after a while headed to Manteo and the courthouse. Swung around a block and ended up parking on Budleigh Street, half a block from the courthouse. Deputy Dorsey was just coming out the side door on Budleigh as I approached, and he held the door open for me. I saw Balls' Thunderbird parked in a reserved spot. I went up the backstairs and met Mabel in her office next to the sheriff's.

"Agent Twiddy and Odell went down to Wanchese a while ago," she said. "They may not be back for a . . ." And then we heard them coming up the backstairs. Balls was saying something to Odell about "two brothers who should know better."

I stepped out into the hall.

"Saw your car outside," Balls said.

"Come on in," Odell said, inclining his head toward his office.

We went in. Odell took a seat behind his desk and Balls and I took the two chairs in front. Odell said, "Agent Twiddy filled me in on everything been happening to you."

I nodded. Turning to Balls, I said, "I got another call last night. He wanted to know if I wanted to smoke another Kool cigarette."

Balls didn't say anything, just looked at me.

The round clock on the wall made a clicking sound.

I tried once more to make light of it. "Maybe he's just trying to, you know, play games . . ."

Balls made the slightest negative shake of his head.

Odell spoke. "Last night I talked with Detective J. W.

Doles over in Rocky Mount. Friend of mine I've known for some years. Told him about the clipping that was on your windshield."

So Balls really had filled in Odell on all the details.

Odell continued. "Doles was very interested. He has no leads at all. Slaying looks so random." He studied his folded hands a moment and then looked back up at me. "It sounds like a stretch, I know, but Doles wondered if maybe this same character who's messaging you, might be the one who did the woman. And leaving you the clipping could be a way of sending you another—more deadly—message."

I think I gave an involuntary shudder. "Scary to think so," I said so quietly it was barely audible.

Odell nodded. "I know." He rubbed a hand across this jaw. "A stretch, true. But not to be ignored. Doles didn't ignore it, and he's plenty sharp."

Balls tilted back in his chair. "Knowing you, you've probably pissed off plenty of people—in the past and in the present, matter of fact."

"No, I can't think of anyone, really. And I've thought about it a lot and I can't come up with anyone I might have pissed off . . . not to that extent."

Odell said, "Obviously this guy knows you from some years back. Not somebody new. The Kool cigarettes and all."

"I still say it's possibly just games with him. After all, he hasn't actually made any threats at all," I said. Whether I believed this was doubtful.

Odell said, "They may not be overt threats, but I think he has, in a way, made threats."

Balls trained his eyes on me. "So do I," he said evenly. He let the legs of his chair settled squarely on the floor with a clunk sound. "Wish you'd hurry up and get outta Dodge."

"Thursday morning," I said.

By Wednesday I was virtually all packed—and even Elly

was. That morning close to noon I put the black canvas cover over my bass and prepared to take it down the stairs and put it in the Subaru Outback. The rear seats were folded forward to make plenty of room. I wrestled the bass down the stairs, and then went back up and got my revolver, checked on Janey and told her I'd see her later. She chirped and did her head bobbing. I locked up securely.

Driving up the Bypass to the swing over to Duck Road, I kept a watchful eye on the traffic. Damn, I'd be glad not to be obsessed with possible a villain.

But maybe my diligence paid off.

For no sooner was I on the Duck Road, following a line of traffic in front of me, than I noticed three cars behind me, a dark Audi sedan keeping pace with the flow of traffic. My sight shifted constantly between the road in front of me and my rearview mirror.

As we got closer to Duck, the speed limit dropped from forty-five to thirty-five, and then abruptly to twenty-five. Traffic slowed and I kept my sights on the Audi, now two cars back since one had pulled off at the Hillcrest beach access.

Approaching Scarborough Faire shopping area, I waited until the last minute to signal my right turn up into the parking area behind the bookstore. After I made my turn I slowed almost to a stop to watch the Audi. It continued straight ahead. Okay, Harrison, just cool it a bit.

When I parked near the walkway, I unloaded my bass—convinced it got heavier each year—and, with the neck of the instrument propped across my shoulder and one hand gripping the side, I carried it to the area where we would play. Dane was already there setting up his drum set, Jim had put music stands out, and Frank had his keyboard almost ready to go.

Betsy Robinson greeted me with a mile-wide smile and an awkward hug around the bass.

"So glad you're going to be with us today, Betsy," I

said.

"Delighted," she said and drew the word out with real meaning.

A small crowd had gathered at the few tables and benches out front. Two children scampered about, and their parents tried in vain to get them under control.

Jim tuned his trumpet to the keyboard. I pulled the cover off of my bass and then began the tuning process while Frank hit a G-note, D, A, and E. I was not far off. The E was a little sharp and the G was a tad flat. Frank nodded when I finished.

Jim looked around at us. Dane sat with sticks in hand, ready to play; Betsy perched one hip on a tall stool up front; Frank had fingers curved above the keys; and I stood, the bass leaning into me. "Okay," Jim said. He tapped his foot, setting the tempo, he counted off, and we opened, as we always did, with a bouncy rendition of "A Foggy Day." A smattering of applause. The crowd had grown by several more people. Into the single mic up front, Jim said, "Thank you, ladies and gentlemen—and youngsters. We're happy to have with us today songstress extraordinaire, Betsy Robinson." He turned to Betsy and asked, as if he hadn't already gotten the word from her. "What'll it be, Betsy?"

She stood, smiling broadly, and came to the mic. "How about 'I've Got a Crush on You'?"

"That'll be great, Betsy," Jim said.

She turned toward Frank and me. "D-flat," she said. Frank nodded.

Jim tapped off a moderate upbeat tempo. Frank played a tasteful four-bar intro, and Dane and I came in as Betsy began to sing. When she finished, the applause was more vigorous. Well, too, there were more people. But she was good, very good.

We played a couple of more instrumental tunes and then Betsy did the vocals on a beautiful rendition of "Autumn Leaves."

While we played, I kept a scan on the audience. Looking for what? A psychotic killer with a sign around his neck proclaiming himself as such? Also, I had glanced more than once back at the parking area at cars coming in and going out.

A couple of minutes before two, we took a short break. I went into Island Bookstore, one of three on the Outer Banks owned by Bill Rickman. Inside, after breathing in the familiar and comforting aroma of the books, I spoke to Cindy and chatted with her a few minutes. It was always fun in there. And she said it had been a nice summer, business had been good. She wanted to know how my writing was coming along and I told her about the upcoming trip to Paris and how I intended to spend some time while there polishing short stories for a book.

When we started playing again, we did "Confessing" and Jim performed a Louis Armstrong-type of vocal on it, plus some mid-range jazz trumpet. Every now and then his playing reminded me of Bobby Hackett's wonderful cornet style. I found myself smiling in appreciation.

Toward the end of our second set, Betsy sang a great rendition of "Come Rain or Come Shine." It was in F, an easy key.

I had mostly forgotten the audience, enjoying the playing, when someone in the crowd caught my attention. Standing alone near the back was a tall man, hands down by his side, a slight smile on his face. He looked to be in his late thirties, maybe early forties, close to my age. He was dressed in slacks and a button-down shirt. He wore a lightweight windbreaker type coat, almost thigh-length. Definitely less scruffy than our usual attire at the Outer Banks. Although I couldn't see his face clearly because of shadows from an overhanging roof, there was something about him that seemed vaguely familiar. I didn't know whether I knew him or had ever seen him.

But there was something about him.

I couldn't tell if he was looking at the band or staring at me.

I started to give a nod in his direction, to let him know I might know him. But I didn't.

Then next to our final tune, Jim introduced Betsy again and asked her to sing "At Last." Again she told us it would be in the key of F.

We started in on it, and her voice rang out true and clear.

I looked at the audience again.

That man was gone.

Chapter Eleven

With the last-minute details of getting ready for Paris, I was busy Wednesday night and so was Elly.

There had been no further "messages" and because of the upcoming trip, I had given less than usual thought to who might be out there posing an unknown threat. Although neither of us had addressed it, I was sure Elly and I both sensed that getting over to Paris would give us a break from the hovering specter of . . . of whoever he was. And Elly would be with me and safe, I felt like. I no longer feared that Martin would be in any danger. Whoever killed the young mother near Raleigh had not bothered her son.

However, I did ask Odell if he could have a deputy swing by Elly's house from time to time, just to show a presence. No problem, Odell said. This made Elly feel a bit better also.

Elly and I had talked briefly at least three times on the phone that night. She confirmed, for probably the umpteenth time, that, yes, she'd checked with her friend Linda Shackleford, a reporter, who had wanted to take us to the Norfolk airport.

After much discussion, we had insisted that she *not* take us all the way to the airport. Instead, we settled on her kind offer to pick Elly and her luggage up and bring her the twenty miles up to my house. That way, I wouldn't have to drive down to Elly's, turn around, and backtrack past my place going north to Norfolk.

I had carried Janey over to Misty's house, along with Janey's seeds and treats and a bag of pellets for the bottom

of her cage. Misty said she was delighted to look after Janey
—as long as I brought back some dark chocolates from Paris.
Absolutely.

Our flight was at eleven-fifty and, since it was international, we needed to be at the airport two hours ahead. I
don't like to jog in the airport, so we scheduled plenty of
time, especially for possible traffic delays, which were always possible on the loop around Norfolk.

At eight-thirty Thursday morning, Linda Shackleford
and Elly pulled into the cul-de-sac. It appeared Linda had
washed her Toyota, a newer hatchback than she used to
drive. She had progressed from taking classified ads to pho-
tographer to fulltime photojournalist on *The Coastland
Times*, doing a good job. She had taken a job with the *Outer
Banks Sentinel*, and I was pleased for her. Then, with the un-
fortunate closing of that paper, she'd gone back with the
Times.

Linda, one of my favorites, grinned widely as she got
out of the car. She's got big teeth that I've always said look
strong enough to chew through rawhide.

Elly emerged from the Toyota and, with Linda assisting,
started getting her luggage out of the trunk. Elly wore com-
fortable-looking slacks and a loose top. She had a folded cotton sweater and a windbreaker over her arm. She stood beside my car until I came around, suitcase in one hand, laptop
in its case in the other, and gave her a kiss on the lips. "Off
on a great adventure," I said.

"Yes," she said, "and I guess I'm always just a little nervous. Bit of travel anxiety."

"Only natural," I said, "but should be a good, boring
flight."

"I like boring," she said.

Linda laughed. "Way I like a flight to be too."

"Let me make a quick run back upstairs, double check,
and be right down," I said. Taking the steps two at a time, I
stepped into the kitchen, glanced around. I had put my bass

on its stand, and went over and loosened the bowstrings. Double-checking the iron bar that secured the sliding glass door I was near the phone when it rang. Grabbed it up.

"Bon voyage," that voice said, and clicked off.

I stood there a beat or two. That son of a bitch knew every move I was making. There was no way I was going to mention this phone call to Elly. Not going to upset her, add to her anxiety.

I took a deep breath, calmed myself as much as possible, put a smile on my face and went back down the stairs. Cheerfully, I said, "Okay, checking: Passports, tickets, supply of euros?"

"All set here," Elly said. Her voice was tinged with a touch of nervousness. I knew she was watching me as I stowed everything in the rear of the Subaru. "You okay?" she said.

"Fine."

We both gave Linda a hug and our thanks.

"I wanted to be a little bit of this trip," Linda said.

There was a touch of wistfulness in her tone; and I had a fleeting moment thinking maybe I should have let her drive us to the airport like she wanted to.

We said our goodbyes, got in our cars, and we were off, on our way . . . to Paris by-way-of Norfolk, a change of planes at Dulles International Airport outside of Washington, and then overnight to Charles De Gaulle Airport in Paris.

Using accumulated mileage, I had secured one business class ticket "free" and an outright purchase for the second. For an overnight flight, it would be much more of a treat for both of us. At least, much less worse.

I saw no sign of the man I'd noticed at the musical gig as we got checked in and through the Norfolk airport with a minimum of difficulty. But I consciously kept glancing around, studying others at the airport. What did I expect, for goodness sakes? That he would show up everywhere I went?

We caught the flight to Dulles, aboard a CRJ, Canada

Regional Jet. A short hop to Dulles. As we took off, Elly held my hand tightly. Time to spare at Dulles, and since we had business class tickets we could have used the airline's lounge, but we didn't.

When we boarded the big Boeing 757 and moved into the business class, Elly was impressed with how much more room we had and that the seats would actually turn essentially into beds. She grinned and played with the seat's controls a bit. I offered the window seat to her, and I took the aisle. Actually, I prefer the window because I'm one of those who likes to look out, whether there's anything to see or not. The flight attendant was friendly and helpful and wanted to know if we wanted something to drink. How nice, we both agreed. I finally began to relax.

When we taxied out on the runway, and got in position for takeoff. I said, "And now we're really off for a new adventure." The engines began to roar and strain against the brakes until the captain let the big aircraft lurch forward, pressing us back in our seats, and we gained more and more speed down the runway. Then we lifted off and we were on our way across the ocean to Paris.

Elly had fun with the seat controls and then with the video and the headset and whether to watch a movie or not. I kept the little map on the video that showed ours progress, ground speed, altitude and location. After dinner—and with real flatware and cloth napkins—the lights were turned down and we prepared to sleep, or pretend to sleep.

I looked over at Elly. She had her eyes closed and I studied her a long time. I thought about the ring I would give her. I wrestled with what the ring would mean. I'd been over this in my mind before, and reached no conclusion. It was more than a friendship ring, of course; was it really an engagement ring?

How would she accept it? I didn't know. Although we had skirted around actually talking about marriage, I knew both of us had mulled it over. Yes, and whether either of us had reached any sort of decision, I wasn't sure.

I mean, I'd even thought about where would we live? Another house? Probably so. What about her mother? And there was Martin; I'd be taking on a responsibility I'd never had before.

I watched her sitting there so close to me, with her eyes closed, and breathing steadily and I thought about the lyrics for that song, and yes, "my cup runneth over with love."

Very gently, I reached my hand across and let my fingers touch her wrist. She opened her eyes and smiled at me . . . with love, and then closed her eyes again.

The air was smooth at thirty-seven thousand feet. A strong tailwind helped push us forward to a ground speed of almost six hundred miles an hour. I watched the little map on the video screen as my eyelids began to get heavy. I felt Elly looking over at me. She patted my arm and touched her head against my shoulder. I didn't think she'd stopped smiling since we smoothed out after takeoff.

Apparently I did fall asleep because when we got into a little rough air I woke up. I saw that Elly was wide-awake and looking at me. Her eyes showed a touch of concern. "Just a bumpy country road in the air," I said. "It'll smooth out shortly." Well, actually it was more like twenty minutes of moderate turbulence before it was like we got back on smooth pavement again. Elly relaxed and went back to her movie. Except for more turbulence approaching Ireland a few hours later, the rest of the flight was smooth.

The flight would take about seven hours, and since the time difference was six hours, we'd land at seven o'clock in the morning Paris time, but our bodies would feel like it was a hell of a short night, since for us it was one o'clock in the morning back home. But I encouraged Elly to reset her watch to Paris time, and forget about what time it felt like it was—as if that could happen.

With an hour or more left on the flight, the cabin lights came on and we caught the aroma of breakfast being readied.

Elly blinked. Her eyes were puffy from sleep, or the lack thereof. She tried to smooth down the back of her hair. I got up so she could go forward to the restroom. It took several tries for her to get her seat back into a non-sleep position so she could get up. We both stifled laughs about her struggle. She took a small cosmetic bag with her. When she came back I could smell that she had brushed her teeth.

It was a good breakfast, with strong coffee, fruit in a cup, a small omelet, a piece of sausage, and a croissant. Yes, a croissant. We were getting closer to Paris.

After breakfast, it wasn't long before I felt us beginning to make a gentle descent. Elly began looking out the window. Just darkness at first. Then, off in the far distance and a break in the clouds, she saw a twinkle of lights. "Oh," she said, pointing. There was an announcement about touchdown in twenty-five minutes. I leaned in close to Elly to peer out the window. The big aircraft began a slow, lazy turn, and we saw more lights, and we were excited. Then in a short while we saw the faraway lights of Paris itself. No wonder it has the moniker of City of Light.

The signal came on to fasten seat belts and we began our final descent. Elly kept her sight out the window the whole time. She reached over and put her hand on my arm as we prepared to land. The monstrous aircraft's tires squealed in protest as we touched down, and the captain slammed on the brakes and engaged the reverse thrust on the engines, slowing the plane sharply enough that you felt the forward push against the seatbelt.

A big grin on her face, her lips a bit pale from a lack of lipstick or balm or whatever else it was that she wore. "We're here," she said, sounding like a kid and I loved her. I realized that completely.

I really loved her.

Chapter Twelve

We gathered belongings we'd carried on, thanked the flight attendants, and joined the rest of the sleepy-eyed flood of people leaving the plane, and followed the signs toward passport control.

Other flights had also come in at this early hour; quite a crowd gathered at passport control. But the lines moved fast and in short order Elly and I were next. We got our passports scanned and stamped and we followed the signs toward baggage claim.

We got our bags and loaded them onto one of the large baggage carts, and went toward the taxi line outside. As we stepped outside, the air was crisp and felt a little damp. It smelled like exhaust from various vehicles. There was noise and chatter, and people either moved rapidly about or stumbled along like they were in a daze. A variety, too, of attire, but most folks looked a little scruffy from long flights. I guess we did too. I automatically ran my hand over my hair, attempting to put some order back to it.

The taxi dispatcher hustled people along, loading them up rapidly. We moved forward, and the dispatcher pointed to a Mercedes off to the left. The driver stood beside the rear of his car, the trunk already open, and we pushed our cart over to him. He loaded the suitcase, but I held on to my laptop case and Elly kept her large soft carry-on bag or purse—or whatever it was. Once inside, I handed the driver a slip of paper on which I had written the address of our apartment, which was to be our home for more than a week.

The driver, a dark-skinned man who appeared very serious, studied the slip of paper, nodded and punched something into a console mounted on his dashboard. He handed the paper back to me, and I held it securely. Not speaking more than a smattering of French, I found such written notes handy.

It was a long trip from the airport to our apartment at 8 rue des Grands Degres, on the Left Bank, across the boulevard from the Seine and Notre Dame. I wasn't sure when, but the taxi fare from Charles De Gaulle Airport to the center of Paris had apparently become a fixed price of fifty-five euros. With the fluctuating exchange rate, that was something like sixty-five or seventy US dollars.

As we got out on the highway, it was obvious that at least half the world was trying to drive into Paris. It was slow going, just inching along, especially in one of the tunnels. I saw Elly nodding sleepily, trying valiantly to stay awake, despite what her body wanted her to do.

Every time I came to Paris it seemed the taxi took a slightly different route getting into the center of town. Finally, the scenery got more familiar and I saw the Seine off to our left and the tubular building of some of the fashion industry across the river. The driver, still silent and serious, worked his way through the traffic to the left turn lane. I was always amazed at the give-and-take attitude of the drivers; virtually no horn honking and no obscene finger gestures.

As we made our turn onto one of the bridges, I nudged Elly and pointed downstream to Notre Dame, visible in the distance. We were both anticipating depression at the sight of the cathedral, so badly damaged in the April fire. But from this distance, it didn't look too bad, as it occupied its regal place there in the middle of the Seine on the *Ile de la Cite.* The Island of the City.

Getting closer to our turn off from Quay Montebello onto a side street to the left, we got a better, but still fleeting, view of Notre Dame. We turned down one block, then left again and another block and we pulled up to the entrance to our apartment; the narrow one-way street was only a block long, with skinny sidewalks on each side.

It was eight-thirty-five. The rental agent, Francois Madet, had emailed that he would meet us at eight-thirty to handover the keys, with another set upstairs in the apartment on the kitchen counter. Madet came bounding down the street from his office several doors away. With his characteristic big smile, he gave us a friendly greeting. We punched in the code for the front door; then there were two gates that needed unlocking. It wasn't really necessary, but he helped us get the three suitcases up the six steps to the tiny elevator. Took us two trips in the lift to the French first floor, which in America we would consider the second floor.

I had stayed in the apartment before, so I was familiar with it. The one-bedroom apartment, bath and a half, was nicely furnished. Two large windows in the living room looked out across the boulevard to the Seine and to Notre Dame. The apartment had belonged to a friend of mine. He had died and I rented now from his son and daughter-in-law.

When Balls, his wife Lorraine, Elly, and I had made our hurried up trip to Paris a year and a half ago, we had stayed at a two-bedroom apartment off St. Germain, several blocks from this apartment, but still just on the edge of the Latin Quarter. I had taken a bit of pride in explaining to Elly that it was called the Latin Quarter because in the olden days, professors in the area had talked to the students in Latin. During that visit, Elly's first, we had taken in all of the usual tourist spots—the Eiffel Tower, the Louvre, Arc de Triumph, and had even taken one of the hop-on/hop-off Big Red Buses around the city. This time, Elly said she wanted mostly to simply people watch . . . a favorite activity of mine as well. Also, she said she would humor me by taking in some of the Hemingway haunts.

"The hero of your youth," Elly had said.

"Well, he is still something of a hero. He worked hard at writing. And I know what that's like."

When we entered the apartment, pushing the bags before us, Francois left us and said he hoped we would find everything in order. I said I was sure we would. Elly went immediately to one of the two big front windows and looked across to Notre Dame. I went to stand beside her.

Elly sighed. "Well, it doesn't look quite as bad as I thought it would . . . at least from here. She leaned her shoulder like a caress against my arm.

"It doesn't look as blunted without the spire as I thought it would."

"Yes, but I was afraid it might look as bad as . . ." She permitted a tiny shrug. ". . . well, as bad as the Cotton Gin up near Grandy . . . only bigger."

Actually, because of large plane trees across the boulevard, we couldn't see the cathedral all that well, and it was obvious that neither we—nor any other curious people—were going to get too close to the cathedral.

There was now a high, secure fence around the building and the garden area in the rear. The solid fence was even topped with coils of razor wire. They were serious about keeping folks out. Scaffolding reached to the sky on the backside. The spire was gone, as we knew from the TV newscasts in the spring. So were the flying buttresses on the side closest to the river. There was at least one flying buttress on the other side. It was hard to tell from here.

People gathered in small groups near the steps that led down to the Seine, taking pictures of Notre Dame, wounded though it was. Later in the day, the used books and posters stalls along the sidewalk would open for business.

Elly turned from the window. "At least it's still there, and I guess from what we can see, it doesn't look as . . . as de-stroyed as I thought it would." Her shoulders sagged a bit. "I guess we ought to unpack?"

I chuckled and shook my head. "No, I think we ought to kick off our shoes and flop down on the bed for a while. Sleep an hour or two . . . then unpack, maybe, and wander out for something to eat."

"I think I'm probably in favor of that, the flopping down on the bed."

We went into the bedroom. She took the side closest to the bathroom. "This okay?" She tested the bed with a push of one hand on the mattress.

"Fine," I said.

"I'm stepping in here a minute first," she said, and went into the bathroom. I used the half-bath near the entrance door in the hall.

Then both of us came back into the bedroom, kicked off shoes, and stretched out. We unfolded the afghan at the foot of the bed and pulled it partially over us. In no time at all, I think both of us were sound asleep.

It was close to noon when we came around, and groggily so. I went into the kitchen and scrounged around for coffee. I made a note of what we'd need to get from the Fran Prix grocery store a block and a half away on Lagrange.

Elly came into the kitchen. She had washed her face and brushed her hair. Lip balm glistened. She tried a smile. "I really need to take a shower, but maybe we'd, I don't know, get something to eat or buy some groceries or something."

I put my arms around her and hugged here close. "We'll just stagger out for lunch—and some strong coffee—then either go to the grocery store or come back and take showers and shop later."

She nodded, and tried again to smile. "I'm not really hungry," she said, "but I could use some of that strong French coffee." Her eyes lighted with a mischievous twinkle, and she reached into her bag she'd had on the plane. "I absconded with two of the croissants from breakfast. Want one?"

I laughed. "Sure."

We ate those and then went downstairs and across the corner from the apartment to Beaurepaire café. We sat outside at one of the little tables near the sidewalk. The early afternoon weather was sunny and very mild. I guessed the mid- to high seventies. There was a clean ashtray on the table. The young waiter came to us. He looked familiar.

He stared at me. "America? Right? Carolina of the North?" His English was good, laced with the pleasing French accent.

"Yes," I said. "*Oui.* I thought I recognized you."

"Came back here month ago," he said. He didn't mention where he had been; at another restaurant, I assumed. He had a neatly trimmed short dark beard and wore black slacks and a nicely starched white dress shirt. "Want to eat? Wine?"

I shook my head and smiled. "*Deux espressos, s'il vous plait.*"

When he left to get our coffees, Elly leaned close to me. "I'm impressed," she said.

At my grin, she added, "With your French."

"Well, you've heard about the extent of it," I said. "I can say please, and thank you, and order two espressos…very little else."

He brought the espressos in tiny cups, tiny spoons, and two tubes of sugar. He also set down two glasses of water that glistened on the outside because the water was good and cold.

"The tap water is very good here," I said to Elly, and we both took big swallows of the water. It tasted excellent.

"Get dehydrated on the plane," she said.

"Yes, drink up."

The espresso was hot and strong. Great. "My cigar," I said. "Would it bother you?"

"Not at all." She smiled. "We're here in Paris . . . live it up . . . sin and all that good stuff." She took a sip of her espresso and touched her lips. "I need this."

I had a fresh Honduran cigar and a case to store it in after a few puffs.

There were only a half a dozen people outside at the café and half of them were smoking cigarettes or vaping.

When we finished our coffees, and spent a few minutes watching people come and go, I stored my cigar in its case, and we prepared to leave. "That shower beckons," Elly said. "Then maybe we'll plan to eat early, pick up a few essentials, and go to bed." She looked at me. "And sleep," she added.

I nodded. "It'll take a day or so to get over the flight and adapt to Paris time."

"Yes, and as soon as we can, I want to call home and let them know we arrived safe and sound."

We crossed the intersection of the two one-way streets and headed to the apartment.

I realized I had not thought about that . . . that stalker, or whatever he was . . . hardly at all since we had landed in Paris. I wasn't going to think about him now, either.

That's certainly what I hoped for, and what I expected. It was a good feeling.

And I wanted it to last.

Chapter Thirteen

Inside the apartment, Elly suggested I take a shower first. "I'll take longer than you will, I expect," she said.

"Okay, but let me show you a little something about that shower before you try to get in." The shower was in a tub that stood a good eighteen inches off the floor. A wooden partition ran the length of the tub's base. "Hold onto this grip as you step up on this ledge and keep hold of it until you feel secure standing in the tub. It can be tricky, and I don't want you falling."

She nodded.

"I'll adjust the temperature, and then you just have to turn this knob."

"I want it good and hot," she said.

"It'll be hot," I said.

"I'll start doing some of the unpacking," she said. "Make any difference which side of the closet, the drawers?"

"Take your pick." I smiled and hugged her. "We're really keeping house for the first time, for a short while anyway," I said. "With Balls and Lorraine it was just sort of camping out."

The shower did feel good and I stood in it for a long time and let the hot water pound against my back. The mirror over the sink had steamed up when I got out and dried off. Went ahead and made a pass at shaving. Would maybe skip shaving tomorrow. If it was good enough for Hemingway . . .

With a towel wrapped around me, I stepped into the bedroom and said, "Your turn."

"You look cute," she said. Her suitcase was open on the

bed and she had almost emptied it, putting her things away. Cosmetics, toothbrush and other items were off to the side; they would go in the bathroom, where there was room over the sink in the double cabinets. I tried to imagine what it would be like to have her little bottles and tubes as a permanent fixture in my bathroom. Not bad, I decided. Maybe even kind of nice.

She took underclothes, her toothbrush, and some cosmetics into the bathroom and slid the pocket door shut. "See you in a little while," she called, a lilt in her voice. In fact, not only was there the lilt but there was also a trace of the Outer Banks accent I loved so much, especially in the word "while." It came out as *"whi-ol"*—the hoigh-toide accent so fast disappearing from all but the native Outer Bankers.

She did take a bit of time in the shower and in the bathroom finishing up. I was dressed and standing at one of the windows in the living room looking out toward the Seine and Notre Dame, watching the people who stopped at the break in the wall; steps lead from that section down to the banks of the Seine. The river was actually not visible from our window because the water is a full story lower than the boulevard in front of us. I thought again of that mechanical voice saying *Bon voyage*, but I pushed it away. We were half a world away from the man who had made that call. Elly would be safe here.

She came out looking like a different person, and I commented on that, complimented her.

"I smell like a different person, too," she said and laughed.

We spent the rest of the afternoon in the apartment, putting our stuff away and familiarizing ourselves with the apartment's various features, such as the dishwasher and the washing machine. The instructions for both were in French and looked much different to me than my Kenmore back home. Although I'd stayed in the apartment before, I'd never bothered with the dishwasher or even the washing machine.

"My French from college isn't doing me that much good," Elly said with a frown as she bent over and inspected the dials on the washing machine. "Oh, well. I'll figure it out."

"Good luck," I said. I did know that the washing machine was a single unit that served to wash the clothes and dry them—at least sort of dry them.

By six o'clock, we started out to eat and pick up a few groceries, and we'd scribbled a list of items.

"We'll be early for dinner," I said, "because the French don't start eating dinner until seven or eight o'clock."

Elly laughed. "That'll be just about bedtime for us."

Shortly before six, we started walking up rue Frederic Sauton, cut right onto tiny Trois Portes, and up around the corner to Lagrange. A marquee for a Chinese restaurant beckoned. "It's nice," I said.

"Sure," Elly said. "Why not come to Paris to eat Chinese food? Makes sense to me."

"Okay, okay." I laughed. "We'll get plenty of chances to eat French food—maybe after we've had Chinese, Syrian, Italian, and Basque right here in our neighborhood."

She laughed too, and held onto my arm.

"Besides," I said, "the Fran Prix grocery store is right across the street."

We were greeted by the young Asian man who, along with his mother, owned the restaurant. He seated us at the little table by the window. There was only one other customer this early, a man who ate alone in one corner. The restaurant had three large aquariums that sparkled cleanly, with plenty of light, and tiny tropical fish drifting and darting about. Your eyes get drawn to the aquariums.

We looked at the menus. The items were listed in French but with English in smaller type underneath the French.

"If you've never had their nems, you must try them," I said.

Peering over the top of her menu, Elly gave me a look.

"You know I've never tried their . . . their whatever." She grinned. "But I've got a feeling I will."

The nems came as appetizers with the meals we ordered —shrimp and some sort of noodles for Elly, and a chicken and fresh pineapple dish for me, with bowls of rice for each of us. In a few minutes, a young Asian woman brought two dinner plates with a tiny bowl of clear sauce set in the middle of each. Then she brought out the nems, still steaming hot. Four thumb-size nems, that looked like small spring rolls, graced each side plate, which also had large leaves of lettuce and sprigs of mint.

Elly said, "I'll watch you."

I took one of the nems, wrapped it in a lettuce leaf, along with two mint leaves, dipped the wrap in the sauce and took a bite. "Good," I said, chewing.

Elly followed the same procedure, took a delicate bite, and nodded appreciatively. She swallowed and said, "You're right, Harrison. They are very good. The sauce helps, too. Sort of vinegary, a little zip to it."

After dinner, we went across Lagrange to Fran Prix and bought a reusable tote bag, a few groceries and coffee, dark roast. Then we went to bed and cuddled quite a bit before drifting to sleep. It was good having Elly in the bed with me, and during the night I waked and reached a hand over to touch her gently to reassure myself she was still there. She stirred when I touched her and mumbled something. I don't know what it was she mumbled but it sounded endearing.

Yes, I could get used to this as a regular way of life. I went back to sleep, and probably with a smile on my face.

Saturday morning we had coffee and croissants and then planned to walk up the two blocks to Place Maubert because she wanted to browse through the farmers' market. Around the city, there were open-air markets on different days of the week. The one at Place Maubert was held on Tuesdays,

Thursdays, and Saturdays, with Saturdays the busiest of all.

There's a touristy restaurant right there at Place Maubert and I told Elly I would sit outside and have another coffee while she went across Boulevard St. Germain to the market. Place Maubert is formed at the intersection of St. Germain, Monge, and Lagrange. Lot of traffic, vehicular and pedestrians. Great people-watching place. It's pretty there, too, because there's a fountain at the tiny square with a low iron fence around the greenery. Different flowers are planted there from time to time.

It was a little strange how some of the people looked so different—so French or attired in other-country fashions. Yet, at the same time, there were some people who looked familiar, like I almost knew them. The waiter brought my coffee and it was more expensive than at other restaurants, attesting to the tourist trade here. Everywhere else in Paris an espresso was two-euros-fifty. Here, it had gone up to three euros. Oh, well, we didn't come to Paris to save money.

I kept glancing across St. Germain to watch for Elly. I knew she was enjoying herself and I was happy about that. While I watched across the street, I saw a man who stood on the curb at the east end of the market.

I sucked in a breath. He looked so familiar, like the man who stood at the back of the audience when we were playing music at Scarborough Faire. I leaned forward, staring, but one of the double-decker Big Red Buses came by just then, slowed for the stoplight and began a slow turn left to go down Lagrange. Making its turn, the bus blocked my line of sight.

The man had disappeared.

Okay, Harrison, cool it. You're seeing ghosts where there are none. I kept telling myself this. After all, we were in Paris, thousands of miles from the Outer Banks.

I finished my now cold coffee, and sat there, casting my eyes about. People-watching wasn't as much fun now, but I was determined to get back in the mood of it. I relit my cigar from yesterday. The first puff or two made me feel dizzy. I held the cigar away a moment. I kept watching for Elly.

Then I saw her near the curb at a rack of clothing. She was listening to something the woman owner was saying to her about the clothes and holding out a top for Elly to inspect.

I felt better, and I went back to my cigar.

Several minutes later Elly made her way across the street at the stoplight and came to my table, a big smile on her face and holding a bag, too. She brought a brown, soft cotton bag with her on the plane and it now bulged with her purchases.

"Look," she said, pulling out a top that had some sort of design woven into the fabric. It was lacy at the top. "Only nine euros and it was made in Italy." She couldn't get rid of the smile. "I'll look real Parisian in this."

There were still more items in the bag, I could tell.

"Oh," she said, "and I got some fruit—tangerines and grapes. They have seeds but they're tasty and the stems are fresh."

We began walking back to the apartment and I thought about how we were keeping house. It was if we were truly a couple. Like a married couple.

I gave thought to that, and I realized I'd been giving more thought to it lately. Earlier in the summer, I had taken one of her rings she wasn't wearing that day—she had slipped it off to do something around her house—and I took the ring to Tim Crank at Creative Jewelers to check the size. I had already talked with him about making a ring with small diamonds and sapphires. Before we'd left for Paris, Tim called to tell me the ring was ready. It was beautiful. A wide band of a ring. Once again, I asked myself what kind of ring it was. A friendship ring? An engagement ring? I hadn't decided, but I planned to give it to her here in Paris. Just waiting for the proper time.

As we walked down rue Frederic Sauton toward the

apartment, she said, "It's such a lovely day, why don't we go to the Luxembourg Garden? We were there for just a few minutes with Lorraine and Agent Twiddy but I'd like to spend some time there, maybe just sitting. Oh, we could get a sandwich from one of the venders and have our lunch there, sitting in the sunshine."

I was happy to see her so upbeat and enthusiastic. "Sounds like a plan," I said. "Put your stuff up and we'll head to Jardin du Luxembourg."

She hooked an arm in mine, and she almost bounced as we walked along.

When we got to the apartment, she washed the grapes and put them and the tangerines in the refrigerator. Then she said, "Oh, we'll take a couple of the tangerines with us . . . and a bottle of water." She went into the bedroom. "Let me just try on this top."

In a moment or two she came back into the kitchen area, where I leaned on the counter. "What do you think?" she asked.

The top, a dark taupe, was rather sheer, especially at the top. I could see her small bra through the material. "Looks great," I said, "especially your bra."

"Oh, I'll wear something under it," she said and twirled around in a mock fashion-like pose.

We walked St. Germain to St. Michel, and then up the long incline of several blocks to one of the entrances to the vast Luxembourg Garden. We went down toward the Senate building and stopped at the fern shrouded fountain of Medici and took pictures. Then we strolled along the graveled paths over past the large round empty bandstand on our left, and I told Elly that they had really good bands there from time to time, including once a rousing big band, playing traditional swing tunes of the 30s and 40s.

She pointed to the big pond down a level from where we were. "Down there?" she said.

"Fine. We'll drag up chairs, into the sun." Chairs were

scattered about. They were made of metal and people moved them about to varied favorite spots.

We went down the wide main steps beyond the wall with its planters, overflowing with flowers and other greenery. Pulling up two chairs into the sun and close to the pond, we watched the children, their toy sailboats gracing the sparkling water of the pond. A couple of sleek radio controlled little boats scooted over the water, guided by handheld controls, usually being operated by a child's father. Sometimes the men let older boys take over the controls. A staff person for the garden told one of the boys to slow his boat down and not be trying to ram the more graceful but slower sailboats. There was a lot of chatter and laughter.

Elly turned to me. "I know it's silly, but it amazes me to hear the little children speaking French. Like how in the world did they learn to be so fluent in a foreign language so young . . . and, oops, it's not foreign to them."

"I know," I said. "I've had the same feeling in the past."

The sun felt good and it was nice just sitting there. Occasionally watching someone saunter by. Elly watched the children with their boats.

Everyone seemed relaxed.

And I was too.

Until I swear I saw him.

He stood near one of the statutes of a woman, off to my left. He was a hundred or more yards away. So it was not the clearest view of him. But it was him—the same gaunt figure I had seen before, standing motionless, arms down by his side. He wore a beige mid-thigh-length coat or windbreaker. He appeared to be staring at me.

I squinted, maybe shook my head to make sure I was actually seeing someone, that this was not just an apparition, some ghost who stalked me.

Then a group of Asian sightseers, led by a woman who held a yellow flag before her, came by between me and the man standing back there. When they passed, he was gone.

Just like that. And just like before. Maybe I was, indeed, beginning to hallucinate. Maybe I was seeing things that didn't really exist. And where could he have gone? Well, there were plenty of places he could have gone. A few steps back or to the left or right and he would be out of my line of vision.

Elly was laughing about something she had seen with the children and their boats and she turned to me to tell me about it, but she looked at my face and stopped mid-chuckle and said, "What's the matter?"

I quickly did my best to smile. "Oh, nothing," I said. "I was just watching that group of tourists."

I don't think Elly believed me. But she didn't press it.

Get a grip, Harrison, I told myself. After all, we were in Paris, for God's sake. A hell of a long way from the Outer Banks.

What sort of a psycho would follow us here?

Chapter Fourteen

That night after dinner we went to be bed early. We started off just cuddling but that quickly grew more intense. A whole lot more intense. Later, as we subsided, we breathed heavily and we both grinned. Elly waved a hand taking in the room, the apartment, all of Paris, and all of our life together. "I like this," she said.

I wrapped an arm around her. "So do I," I said. And I thought about when would be the right time to give her that ring.

Sunday morning, we slept later than usual, then ate a light breakfast before leaving the apartment and heading up Quay Montebello to the bridge behind the fences at Notre Dame, Pont Archivechie. For some time, there had been thousands of locks put on the bridge's grills by lovers, until the city decided they were getting out of hand and adding too much weight to the railings. We crossed that bridge and angled off to the right, to the mostly pedestrian bridge toward trendy Ile St. Louis.

We wanted to see the street performers who were there every Sunday. We weren't disappointed. We could hear the music in the distance even before we saw the players as we passed by the fence that separated all of us from getting closer to Notre Dame. We stopped to look at the backside of the cathedral. Temporary flying buttresses had been erected on the left of the cathedral, and the original ones were intact on the right side. Even though the sun was out and it was a pretty day, there was something very forlorn about Notre Dame.

We couldn't really see the fire damage. We weren't that close. But you could tell something was not right. Something was gone. The people, for one thing. You used to always see people around the church and in the garden area behind it. Now no one was visible. There was only that skeleton-like scaffolding on the left side that reached higher than the cathedral itself.

We turned away from Notre Dame and headed toward the music, as if being drawn by something more joyful.

And joyful music indeed it was. Made me feel at home. A little jazz combo played American tunes, and played well and with a good strong beat. We went closer. The musicians had set up at the end of the pedestrian bridge. The combo consisted of an old spinet piano, a trumpet player, guitar, and drummer (with one cymbal and snare drum) and a very good young bass player. Watching the bass player's left hand and the way he arched his fingers over the strings, I could tell he'd had a lot of classical training.

They were playing a fast, bouncing oldie, "Exactly Like You." About a dozen strollers stopped and listen to them. When the tune ended, there was a smattering of applause, and one middle-age man, grinning, put some coins in the trumpet player's open case that was on the pavement in front of them. They played another tune that started with a riff by the trumpet player. He looked to be in his early fifties; so were the drummer and the piano player. The guitarist and bassist were younger, late twenties or so. Elly and I stood there and listened to them through that improvised tune and we applauded when they finished, and I put in a few euro coins—which are in denominations of from two euros down. No paper bills smaller than a five-euro note. I liked their coins.

Elly and I moved slowly along while the musicians took a short break and talked to each other in French.

Trying not to be too obvious about it, I kept scanning the people . . . just in case. So far, so good.

In chalky white face, gloves, tight fitting clothing, and a little red hat, a mime performed. His only prop was a small wooden stool, which he appeared to be addressing as if it were his sweetheart. While no Marcel Marceau, he was good, and he made Elly and me smile and applaud and get rid of a few more euros.

When the mime finished, four line-skaters set up cones spaced a couple or so yards apart in the middle of the bridge; then they took turns skating faster and faster, weaving in and out along the line of cones.

And a comic performed riding in circles at the far end of the bridge on a bicycle that kept losing parts—until he was left with only a unicycle, which he rode very well, though wobbly, with a look of absolute terror on his face. His act delighted five or six children who watched.

Elly saw a young couple with two small children eating ice cream cones. "I want one," she whispered to me.

For a moment, I thought she meant children. Then I forced my heart out of my throat and realized what she was talking about.

I pointed to the ice cream shop just off the bridge. Several people waited in line at the shop. "Come on," I said. "Best ice cream in Paris."

Later on, we came back to our side of the Seine, went up to the apartment to make a phone call. Using the apartment's landline, I called Yves and Christine Bru, friends of mine of several years, who had urged me via email to go with them for a trip to Bruges, Belgium. They wanted to make it an overnight trip in their car. We planned to leave around nine o'clock Tuesday. It would take us only about three hours to make the trip. They hadn't been to Bruges for more than twenty years; I had zipped through the medieval city a number of years earlier, too, and I knew it would be a great treat for Elly, whom they had not yet met.

I didn't tell Elly about the planned side trip to Bruges until just before we left the Outer Banks for Paris. She was, indeed, excited about the idea. "I'll soon be a world travel-er," she said. "Thanks to you, Harrison."

That Sunday afternoon after I talked with Yves and Christine—whose primary home is in the country well south of Paris but spend the winter in a small apartment on the Ile St. Louis, about a twenty minute walk from our apartment— Elly and I talked about our plans for Monday.

"I know you'll want to pay your respects to some of the Ernest Hemingway haunts. Do that tomorrow?" She chuckled. "At least *start* them tomorrow. Lots and lots of haunts."

I took her hand again. "Appreciate your tolerating me," I said.

So Monday morning we got out fairly early. The weather was nice. We only needed light jackets and might very well do without them as the day wore on. Walking up to Place Maubert, we crossed the busy intersection and wended our way up Monge. Several blocks later we were at the little square at Place de la Contrescarpe.

"The whole city is ancient, of course," Elly said, "but I read that this area was especially active in Roman times." She pointed to one of the narrow streets off the square. She smiled. "That's the direct road to Rome."

"All roads lead to etcetera, etcetera . . ." I said.

We went around the corner and a couple of doors down to 74 rue du Cardinal Lemoine.

Hemingway and Hadley's first apartment, a walkup on the fourth floor. A small metal plaque in French commemo-rated that this was the apartment of American novelist Ernest Hemingway and his first wife.

I looked at the building. A travel agency occupied one of the floors. I thought about them living there and how he was trying to learn to write, and that she spent hours playing an old piano there with great vigor trying to keep warm.

I held Elly's hand. "That was 1920 or 1921. A hundred

years ago. That's hard to believe, and I still think of him as a young man and the two of them living there." I shook my head. "But I have a harder and harder time trying to imagine it, the way it was then."

I knew Elly watched my face.

I got a bit more cheerful. "Just across the street and down a few doors, James Joyce and his family had an apartment at one time." I couldn't help it; I added somewhat softly, "All those years ago."

"Do you want to go to any of the other places?" she asked, lightly squeezing my hand. "Those cafés?"

I managed another smile. "You mean Aux Deux Magots, La Closerie des Lilas, and Lipps? Maybe some others?" I shook my head. "No, not really. I've been there, and, as I said, I have a difficult time trying to imagine what it was like when . . . well, back then."

I stopped rather abruptly there in the middle of the sidewalk. Elly turned toward me, eyebrows raised in question.

"No, that's not so," I said. "I *can* imagine what it was like back then. At times I can really almost *live* it. Make it real. But that's usually when I'm not standing here actually looking at the places where it occurred." I gave an ain't-you-silly kind of shrug. "I guess my fantasies are more powerful when I'm not face-to-face with reality."

We started walking away from 74 rue du Cardinal Lemoine and went around by the outdoor café at Contrescarpe and headed down toward the main Latin Quarter.

After a moment, Elly said, "I used to have trouble keeping up with you . . . what you're thinking . . . the way your mind works." Playfully, she bumped me with her elbow. "But I'm getting better at it."

I wanted things to be festive again, so I said rather loudly and with determined joviality, "Okay, let's go look at some souvenirs and such in the Latin Quarter. You've got to get something for your coworker and for Mabel, you said."

She got a lively skip to her walk. "That'll be fun."

Twenty minutes later we crossed St. Jacques and eased on to one of the narrow, hurly-burly streets in the heart of the tourists-packed Latin Quarter. We were assailed by piped in music from somewhere; the music became so much a part of the overall atmosphere that you hardly separated it from the other sounds of human activity.

Proprietors of gift and souvenir shops stood in their doorways and beckoned all to enter.

Operators of gyro eateries, with the large shanks of meat hanging from a hooks, busily shaved off slivers of meat for sandwiches, and looked up from their serious endeavors long enough to flash welcoming smiles to prospective customers. We passed a shop in which a cook worked near the front window creating crepes, whose sweet aroma brought a smile to our faces.

Elly looked around and grinned. "Like a day at the fair," she said. She pulled on my hand to step toward racks of berets, bags, and T-shirts that spilled out to the edge of cobblestones.

Lightly fingering one of the berets, she appeared to have another thought. "Why don't we go on to your bookstore and then come back here? It might take me a few minutes."

"No rush," I said. "And we won't be at the bookstore long. Do want to stop in to speak to Brian, pay my respects."

We held hands and started up the wide paved area behind the large church, smilingly weaving in and out among other strollers. The bookstore Elly referred to was the Abbey Bookshop, owned and operated by Brian Spence.

Just beyond the block-long area behind the church, there's an alley of a street named rue de la Parcheminerie, and the Abbey Bookshop is crammed right there. Always there's a reasonably fresh pot of coffee sitting on a tiny table outside on the sidewalk, where a number of books are piled also. Potential customers and browsers are invited to have a cup of the coffee.

Brian Spence stood in the doorway. He had just finished

talking to a book buyer who had three volumes tucked under one arm. Brian sells new and used books, virtually all in English. And there are thousands of them in the narrow shop on the street level and more down a narrow stairway to the basement area. Name a book you want, and Brian can invariably put his hands on it. Don't know how he does it, how he remembers where all of these books are.

As Elly and I approached, Brian waved a greeting. He's a tall, handsome man with a good face, open and frank. "Want some coffee?" he called.

Brian was originally from Canada. He told me once he was working on his doctorate in English literature at a college in New York when he got to thinking that after he got his advanced degree he could spend his life teaching freshmen composition—or he could open a bookshop in Paris.

That was thirty years ago.

Good choice.

We shook hands and I introduced him to Elly. He wanted to know how long we would be in Paris.

"Until Sunday," I said.

"When are you going to write a book set in Paris?" he said. It was a bantering question he had asked me before.

"Maybe the next one," I said, as usual.

Elly browsed through the books stacked outside. She found one touted as being a guide to working crossword puzzles and, smiling, she picked it up and held on to it. Then there was one on knitting. "Mother or Mabel would like this," she said. While Brian and I chatted, she found an historical novel called *After the Revolution*, and added that to her collection.

Before we left, I asked Brian about a copy of one of Harlan Coben's mystery novels. He went right to an almost new soft-cover edition of the book. As I was settling the bill with a young woman tucked away in a tiny alcove that contained a cash register and computer, a bearded man came in and, after speaking to Brian, squeezed his way past me. He was followed by two college-age women. I heard one of them say to Brian they had been told his shop was like Shakespeare and Company used to be.

I tended to agree with them.

Shakespeare and Company was so famous and so popular that it was now always crowded to overflowing. Lots of people outside the bookstore posing for pictures with the sign overhead in the background. Heck, there was now even a coffee and pastry shop attached to the store's structure. Oh, well, it was still Shakespeare and Company and its predecessor, the original bookstore that Sylvia Beech operated in the 1920s and beyond, carried such a golden history of Hemingway, Fitzgerald, Ezra Pound, James Joyce, and others, the popularity couldn't be ignored. Yes, it was justified.

But now I liked the intimacy of the Abbey Bookshop.

Brian gave us a used bag to put our books in. We bade him goodbye and promised to stop by again during the week and see him.

"Those souvenirs for you," I said to Elly as we started toward the hustling streets in the Quarter.

She didn't take long at all in picking out a black beret, adorned with a removable silver replica of the Eiffel Tower. "This should be touristy enough for Becky," Elly said. She also bought a nice bag for Mabel that had a zipper closure and was imprinted with a picture of Notre Dame, pre-fire, on one side and a scene of the Seine on the other.

"A late lunch?" I said.

"Yes, by all means. I've worked up an appetite with all this walking."

Actually, she almost always had a good appetite but never appeared to gain an ounce. I thought about her body and how nice it was.

"What are you thinking?" she said, dodging a couple who appeared dead set on running into us.

I realized I was smiling. "Oh, nothing," I said. "Just thinking about how nice it is to be here with you."

We crossed St. Jacques again and headed toward Square Rene Viviani, which contained the ancient tree that still hung on after more than four hundred years.

"The Tea Caddy?" I said, pointing to the little café with leaded glass windows. A sign outside said the café had been in operation since 1928.

Elly got a quiche with salmon and I opted for their eggs Benedict, always a good choice there. The server, a tiny French woman and one of the new owners, brought us a carafe of chilled water and Elly ordered English breakfast tea, at my suggestion. I knew she would love the way it was served with the antique silver leaves strainer, the whole ritual.

After we ate and signaled for the check by discreetly holding up my credit card. With a smile and a chirping of French, the woman brought the little hand-held credit card reader to the table. She ran the scanner and handed back my card. It was nice not to have to let it out of my sight. I left a few euro coins, even though gratuity is figured in the bill

"Shakespeare and Company is just around the corner," I said. "I guess we ought to stop by there. Take a quick look."

As expected, a dozen or more people were in front of the bookstore, several of them taking pictures. I peeped in the door. Big crowd inside. Two young people, a man and a woman, handled sales behind a high counter. At my insistence, Elly posed for a picture with the Shakespeare and Company sign and entrance behind her.

We cut through the square to head to the apartment. After we had gone a short distance, Elly said, "I see what you mean by the crowd." With a tilt of her head, she indicated she meant Shakespeare and Company.

"But still," she said, "there's a certain—what?—mystique or maybe magic about it, about seeing it and knowing how it figured so much, especially like you've said, with Hemingway, and Fitzgerald, and James Joyce . . ."

"Yes," I said, "because of that we can forgive the many

people who want to see it, and who crowd it."

She grinned big. "Like us."

As we got closer to the apartment—only about three blocks away—Elly said, "I think I'm ready to prop by feet up a while." Then, "Oh, I know we need to pack for tomorrow . . . but that won't take long. We can do it later." She smiled up at me and took my hand.

I thought about the ring. Later this afternoon, maybe. Yes, we could go across the street, sit at Beaurepaire. I'd present her with the ring. Sort of formally.

"This is all so nice, isn't it?" Elly said.

I punched in the code for our building's front door. "It's wonderful." I thought about how nice it was to be in Paris and away from the nutcase who was stalking me. *Surely that couldn't have been the guy I glimpsed at Luxembourg Garden. Just my active imagination.*

I added, "And it's so . . ." I started to say "safe," but I just let the sentence die, and said again, "wonderful."

Chapter Fifteen

We did put our feet up when we got into the apartment. In fact we kicked our shoes off and stretched out on the bed. Both of us dozed a while. Later, I got up, went in the bathroom and splashed cold water on my face. I heard Elly beginning to stir also.

"I went sound to sleep," she said when I came into the bedroom. She sat on the edge of the bed, flexing her shoulders.

"Coffee?" I said. "Across the street? Shot of espresso?"

"I'm drinking more caffeine than I'm used to," she said, "but it doesn't seem to bother me."

"We're burning it up," I said and touched her shoulder and then massaged the back of her neck.

"Feels good," she mumbled. "Let me run in there and then we'll go if you want to."

In less than ten minutes we locked up the apartment, and stood waiting for the elevator door to open. Elly gave me a look. "Are you up to something, Harrison?"

"What in the world makes you think that, Elly?"

The elevator door opened and we stepped inside. She kept her eyes trained on me. "I just know you," she said.

I shrugged and smiled. "Let's have an espresso."

We took the elevator down to the foyer, and started across the street for an espresso and to do a little people-watching. But my main purpose was the ring. It was in its nice little case and stuck secretly in the right-hand pocket of my slacks.

The weather remained mild and sunny. As we crossed

the intersection, I could see the couch and table outside the café were vacant. A comfortable place to sit and still be outside. Really a two-person loveseat. On colder days, there was an electric heater well above the couch that could envelope you in a flow of warm air. There were about fifteen other tables with chairs under the awnings. The outdoor terrace was encased on the sides with clear glass sliding walls. The front of the outdoor section was open to the sidewalks. Seating was also available inside.

We took the couch and moved pillows to the small of our backs. "This is great," Elly said. She lifted her chin. "A view of the world from right here."

She was happy and so was I. It seemed a perfect time for the ring.

Then the young waiter we knew came up with a book in his hand. "A friend of yours came today and required—requested—this book I give you. From him."

I stared down at the collection of Hemingway's short stories.

Suddenly, this was not the time to give Elly the ring, or to think about anything else—except this book.

And who left it for me. Just like that, I didn't feel good at all.

Elly started to say, "Well isn't that nice that . . ." Then she saw the look on my face and her sentence died, and so did the happiness in her eyes.

I took the book and mumbled, *"Merci."* I turned the book over in my hands. There was a piece of paper like a bookmark visible. I opened the book to the mark. It was "Hills Like White Elephants."

Being careful to touch it only on the edges of the note, I stared at what was written. In block letters there were three words: "Better be careful."

I closed the paper and shut the book.

Elly watched my face.

The young waiter stood there. "Espressos?" he said.

I nodded. "Please," I said in English. Then I asked, speaking slowly and trying to enunciate clearly, "What did this person look like? This person who gave you the book?"

The waiter gave the hint of a Gallic shrug but smiled his answer: "Like an American," he said. Then he added, "Tall," he said. "Your size. He wore khaki pants. A jacket." He swept his hands along his sides to demonstrate that it was a fairly long jacket. Probably mid-thigh.

Light tan or khaki-colored slacks would tag him as probably American. The French invariably wore dark or black trousers or jeans.

"Did he have a beard? Long hair, short hair?"

"I don't remember. He showed me a picture on his telephone of you and madam . . . together. And I said I would do, and I was busy." He tilted his head toward me again. "Deux espressos?"

"Yes. Sorry," I said.

He hurried away.

I took a deep breath. Elly remained silent, waiting. Now it was definitely time to tell Elly about my suspicions, tell her all of it, stuff that I had left out in the past before we left the Outer Banks. "Elly," I said, and I took her hand, "I'm afraid that . . . that nutcase, whoever he is, has followed us to Paris." I paused and she leveled her eyes at me.

"Go on, Harrison. Continue."

"Well, I didn't want to alarm you unnecessarily and I wanted to be sure, be sure that I wasn't being paranoid."

There was no question now about the look in her eyes. She was determined, solid, stoic, and angry with me.

"I know, Harrison. You were playing the big macho man and protecting poor little me from worrying." She leaned closer, "But damnit, I'm not a kid. I'm a tough Outer Banker and I can handle myself and any . . . any son of a bitch who comes along."

It was about the first time I'd heard Elly cuss, even mildly so.

The waiter brought our espressos and two glasses of water. I took a big swallow of the water. My throat felt parched.

There was no question in my mind but that she could handle most any son of a bitch who came along—but maybe not one so clever and devious as this one.

"Okay," I said. "Balls, Agent Twiddy, believes, as I do now, that this character, for some reason that I don't know, that Balls doesn't know, is obsessed with me, and eventually wants to do me harm." I stopped and squeezed Elly's hand. "He may even want to harm you as a way of getting back at me."

I told her about feeling like I had seen someone who might be this person here in Paris, and at the music job we played at Scarborough Faire, and more cigarette butts, the whole thing.

And now this book.

As if reading my mind, Elly tilted her heard toward the book, which I had laid on the table beside my espresso. "Why this book?" she said.

I put half of the small tube of sugar in my espresso, stirred with the tiny silver spoon, and took a sip. Delaying? Maybe. "The story deals with pregnancy and the possibility of an abortion—even though neither are ever mentioned in the story. The hills like white elephants, I think of as a symbol of a stomach swollen with child. Literary stuff."

"And the note?" she said.

"I figure it's a reference to our, you know, sleeping together. Better be careful or you'll get pregnant. At least that's the way I read it. He knows what the story is about. He's obviously heard me talk about it in the past . . . some time, somewhere. I have no idea when."

She got a wry, but almost bitter twist to her mouth. "He may know a lot about you if he is someone from your past, but he must not know you've had a vasectomy."

It surprised me that she would get that straightforward,

that biological. My late wife had been terrified of getting pregnant; thus the vasectomy years earlier to try in vain to appease her. Now, I couldn't tell whether Elly really resented that I had the operation. Did she maybe unconsciously yearn for another child, with me as the father? Maybe she hadn't been thinking of ice cream earlier, after all.

"So, what do we do now?" she said. The practical, let's-get-tough Elly was coming to the surface; a facet of hers I had not seen before. I was impressed, I must admit.

"We call Balls. He made me swear to keep him informed."

"What do you think Balls can do from over there . . . when we're way over here?" That was one of the first times I heard Elly refer to my long-time SBI friend as anything but Agent Twiddy.

"Not sure, other than give advice, but he also knows some lawmen here, too, from past conferences and at the FBI's Quantico facility."

She nodded and took a sip of her espresso, frowned, and tore open the tube of sugar and poured it all in the coffee, stirred vigorously, splashing a few spills into the saucer; she tried another sip. Half of her espresso was gone.

After staring at her coffee cup for a moment or two, she trained her eyes on me. "What sort of person would this be? Think about it. He's obsessed with you . . . for some reason. Maybe hates you? Wants to rattle you, get under your skin, and maybe—as you say—do you or me or both of us harm. But you're not sure. Yet, at any rate."

I listened to her. These were thoughts I'd mulled over too, and it was good to hear Elly voicing the same sentiments.

She said, "And obviously he doesn't have anything else to do but follow you around." She pursed her lips, thinking. "That means he doesn't have a regular job—but has plenty of money. Hops a plane and comes to Paris."

I was quietly agreeing with everything she said.

"And with the cigarettes, which you haven't smoked for years, and even the Hemingway story . . ." She tilted her head toward the book. ". . . indicates that he's known you a long time, that there's something that goes back years."

She pushed her empty cup away. "Let's do it," she said. "Let's call Balls." Then, "What time is it back home?"

"Decent hour," I said, and put a five-euro bill on the table, waved at the waiter, and said, "*Au revoir. Merci.*"

Back in the apartment, I went to the landline. The phone was Internet connected and we could make calls without the long-distance charges. I could have also used my cell phone, which I had enabled for use while in Paris. Cost a bit but was worth it, I figured.

I punched in 001 and Balls' cell number. It rang four times, and I was beginning to think Balls might not pick up because he wouldn't recognize the number. But he answered, and this time with an uncharacteristic almost polite "Hello" instead of his usual gruff "Yeah?"

"It's me, Balls. Weav . . . and we may have a problem, Houston." A little astronaut phrase to ease into what I was about to tell him.

He listened while I went into quite a bit of detail about thinking I had sighted a person here I had seen in Duck and then about the book this afternoon.

He was quiet. So quiet that I thought for a moment we might have lost the connection.

But then he said, "Shit." And I knew Balls was back with me. "Yeah, Houston, I do think we have a problem. Wish to hell I was over there too. No way I can swing it, though."

Then he said something I didn't like to hear at all. "Besides, by the time I could get there, he might have already made his move."

Elly sat close to me on the other stool at the kitchen counter. She could probably hear Balls' end of the conversation because I moved my head toward her.

I said, "I don't think he's ready yet to . . . to make his move, as you say. Still sort of playing with me."

"Probably right," Balls said. "His idea of foreplay. But you got to be ready for action, and I don't know how you're gonna do it over there." He made that humpf sound of his. "If you went to the French police, what'd you tell 'em? 'Hey, there's somebody kind a bugging me.' That'd really get some action going." The sarcasm came through loud and clear.

Then he shifted gears and asked, "When you coming home?"

"We're scheduled to fly out Sunday. Almost a week from now."

As if to himself, he mumbled, "Wish you were coming back sooner."

At the moment, I did too. "Tomorrow," I said, "friends of mine have invited us to ride with them to Bruges, Belgium. Stay overnight, and come back Tuesday."

"Riding in their personal car?"

"Yes."

"That'd be best." A pause of a beat. "Surely that bastard won't be following you there."

"I wouldn't think so either."

"But he'll be waiting for you when you return."

Chapter Sixteen

Tuesday morning the sun was out, and from what I could see of the sky between the buildings when I stepped briefly outside, there was hardly a cloud visible. We had spent Monday night close to the apartment; we fixed a light dinner and went to bed early.

I don't think either of us had slept well. We couldn't rid our minds of the fact that this—this stalker, or whatever he was—was here in Paris and was watching us, knew our schedule. Keeping tabs on us. Tormenting us. And getting closer. There had been no hint of violence yet, but I feared there would be, eventually. He wasn't doing this and then just letting it go. He wanted me to know he was after me and he wanted me to fret and worry.

And I was fretting and worrying. Not just for me, but for Elly too.

When it was close to the time for Yves and Christine to arrive, I came back downstairs and brought to the sidewalk the small overnight suitcase Elly and I had packed with both of our needs, which were amazingly few. No need to bring anything fancy to wear.

It was about seven minutes to nine and Elly would be locking the apartment and coming right behind me. I glanced back through the glass in front of the door and saw the light come on in the short hall near the elevator; so Elly was on her way.

Naturally, I had looked both ways along our street when I first came out, making sure no one lurked about. At the far end of the block, a woman I had seen before walked slowly with her leashed small dog. The dog stopped frequently to sniff out the latest news, and she seemed in no hurry at all.

I punched in the code for the heavy oak front door. I held open the door for a smiling Elly. She said, "*Merci, monsieur.*"

"And we're off on another adventure," I said.

She made a dramatic show of scrutinizing our surroundings, including the rooftops of the buildings around us. "And no Evil One in sight."

It was an effort for her to put on a show of high spirits, but maybe not too much. Knowing her, she was determined to enjoy our trip to Bruges. As usual, she had read a great deal about the old city in preparation for the trip. She was, I reminded myself, a history major in college, a passion she continued—along with her long addiction to crossword puzzles.

Elly was dressed in dark gray tailored slacks. They were trim but looked comfortable for traveling. She wore a long-sleeved blue shirt, somewhat mannish looking, and a light-weight cotton sweater over it. We both carried jackets for a bit of warmth that we might need at night.

It was a couple of minutes before nine. Two panel trucks came by and squeezed around the corner at the far end of our street. A Toyota SUV passed, and then I saw Yves' silver-gray Peugeot sedan approaching from the right. There were no vehicles behind him. Good, because he had to stop long enough for us to put our overnight bag in the trunk, and get in.

When he stopped, both Yves and Christine stepped out to greet us, leaving the doors of the car open. At least Yves stepped out; Christine hopped out. A birdlike, wisp of a woman in her sixties, she moved quickly, using one hand to brush back hair that always seemed to be coming loose from a braid at the back. Yves was a tall, handsome man with a mustache, and kindly eyes. He wore a tweed sports coat over a sweater and button-down shirt.

I introduced them to Elly. We all exchanged handshakes and *bises*, the light kisses to each side of the face.

Still holding my hand, Christine chirped her head toward Elly. "She's pretty."

Yves, a trace of smile and looking appraisingly at Elly, nodded his head with approval.

Elly actually blushed, shifted about, and mumbled, "Thank you . . . thank you."

I had met Yves and Christine through the late owner of the apartment. He is semiretired as a financial consultant and architectural historian. Jointly, he and Christine are writing an exhaustively researched tome on an eighteenth century hotel/residence on I'l St. Louis.

I knew Elly would find Yves knowledge of the history and architecture of the city fascinating.

Another car came up behind us, the driver waiting patiently for us to get the bag in the trunk, along with jackets that were not needed now. Christine insisted I sit in the front passenger seat; Elly sat in the back with Christine, who would serve as our navigator.

Both Yves and Christine spoke English but I had to listen very carefully to be able to understand them. They had the same difficulty, apparently, when Elly and I talked, and I tried to remember to speak slowly and very distinctly, avoiding strictly American idioms.

We headed toward the beltway that encircles the city and then exited onto what Yves said was the "Motorway we want." Yves drove smoothly, shifting gears with fluidity, merging in and out of the traffic with amazing politeness from other drivers as well. Yves commented on several of the buildings we passed, telling us what they were. I only understood a couple of them. Elly leaned slightly forward so she could hear Yves more clearly. I knew she found it most interesting.

Christine kept a chatter going with Elly. Twisting around in the seat I stole a glance at Elly. She smiled at

Christine and occasionally managed a short comment to let Christine know she understood and was listening. Shortly, we left the city behind us and we cruised along on a very fine highway. The big trucks we came upon all stayed to the right. I could see the beginning of farmland. The squares and rectangles of neatly tended acreage were arranged in orderly fashion. Stretched across one field were dozens of power-generating windmills, their great arms extended like metal giants from another planet.

We began to see large overhead signs of upcoming cities and towns and finally the name Bruges. When we were about an hour from Bruges, we stopped at a fueling station and restaurant combination; took restroom breaks and got a light lunch. It was really essentially a fast-food place, so we weren't too thrilled.

In no time at all it seemed, we started into the outskirts of Bruges and drove slowly on the narrow streets crowded with pedestrians and bicycles, and an occasional car or a small delivery truck.

"I believe everyone here is young," Elly said as she eyed two couples we cased past.

"This is a place very popular," Yves said. He alternated between looking out for pedestrians and eyeing the GPS display on his phone. We were trying to locate the hotel where Yves had made reservations. Christine sat with an open map in her hands and kept a constant flow of directions to Yves. "*Gauche, gauche*," she said. Left, left.

Instead, Yves turned right.

"No, no," Christine said.

But there in front of us on the right was Martin's Hotel Brugge, the one we were looking for. Christine did the Gallic shrug and put her map away.

Yves pulled to a little space in front of the hotel, engaged the hazard lights on the Peugeot, and we hurriedly got out, opened the trunk and I put the two suitcases and one other bag of Christine's out on the sidewalk. A young couple had to maneuver around the bags to get past us on the sidewalk.

"Wait for me in the lobby," Yves said, and he dashed inside to inquire about parking. We started in as Yves came back out. "They told me where I can park the car. I'll be back quick."

The lobby was small but there were a couple of comfortable stuffed chairs and a two-person sofa. Glass doors opposite the entrance looked out to neatly laid out courtyard, complete with two white tables and chairs, a small fountain. I moved our suitcases to one side. Christine and Elly sat on the sofa. I stood and looked around. Two attractive and animated young women tended the registration desk. They smiled in our direction. I assumed they knew we waited for Yves.

Ten minutes later Yves came striding in the door of the hotel. He waved a greeting to us—and spoke to Christine in French; I caught something about parking and distance—and then he and I went to the front desk to register.

The room Elly and I had assigned to us was just off the lobby, up three steps onto a three-by-three foot "porch" and the door to the room. A big heavy brass key unlocked the door. A lovely room, dominated by a queen-sized bed complete with a white lacey canopy.

"Wow," Elly said. "This is nice."

"The bed looks almost wicked," I said.

"Um-huh. Cool it, Lothario." But she grinned with delight. She checked out the bathroom and its big white porcelain fixtures. Gold-colored faucets. Plenty of towels, soap and shampoo.

We had agreed to meet Yves and Christine back in the lobby in twenty minutes to explore the downtown area. Yves had suggested, too, that we take a boat tour of the canals that lace the city. Wonderful idea, we said.

When the four of us stepped out of the hotel's automatic doors onto the sidewalk, Yves pointed to our right. A few doors away, a relatively wide street spilled almost to over-flowing with strolling sightseers. No one seemed to be in a hurry.

And we were in no hurry. We wanted to take in the sights, peep into the shop windows, smile at the people who smiled in return. Smell the chocolate. Lots and lots of chocolate. Every other store appeared to be a chocolate shop. At one window, Elly stopped and, with a big smile, touched my arm and pointed at a sign in the window. "I agree," she said.

The sign read: "A balanced diet is chocolate in both hands."

We made our way to the main canal and bought tickets for a boat tour. A set of concrete steps led down to a docking area. Several people waited there for the next boat. We got in line and stood there in the sun. It was warm and we didn't need our jackets.

In a few minutes an eighteen or twenty-foot open boat loaded with customers pulled up to the dock and the people began to disembark. The captain helped them over the gun-wale. Some of the people tipped the captain. He looked the part: He was a big man with a gray beard, a big smile, and sported a Greek fisherman's cap, perched at something of a rakish angle.

When the last couple struggled out of the boat, the captain began collecting tickets as he helped those of us in line to board. Bench seats lined each side of the boat. The diesel engine idled nicely and I could smell the exhaust. It was not unpleasant. The four of us sat together on the star-board side, up fairly close to the wheel. Altogether there were probably close to twenty of us. The captain freed the one thick line from a cleat on the dock and climbed aboard. The boat rocked gently.

He flipped a switch on the console that obviously en-gaged the microphone he held in his left hand. With his right, he advanced the throttle a tad and steered us away from the dock. "Welcome aboard!" he boomed. "Everyone comfortable?" A few enthusiastic "yeses."

We moved steadily, but not fast into the canal, and the captain began a running commentary on the buildings, houses, and other attractions that came into view. He spoke in heavily accented English and then switched to French and once to German. We passed large, white, bored-looking swans that treated us with frank indifference. Many of the houses and buildings appeared as though they had been built into the water. I wondered how damp they might be inside. We went under three arched stone bridges. A really tight fit. In one I could have reached out and touched the stone.

At a wide area at one end of the canal, the captain idled the boat into neutral, then an easy reverse, and we turned around to head to the other end of the canal. As the boat backed into the breeze I could smell the diesel again. I could smell the water too and the dampness of bricks and stones, an antique odor that extended generations into the past.

When we finished the canal boat tour and docked at our starting berth, the captain helped each of us exit. I shook his hand and tipped him. Elly wanted to get a picture of me with the captain. He obliged with a big grin.

Then we eagerly made our way toward the chocolate shops.

I was silent as we strolled along, my mind working. I was enjoying the day so much. If life could be this pleasant, why in the world did I write about murder and mayhem? Go back to the kind of writing I did in the beginning. More of the so-called "literary" novels. Okay, I know why I wrote about murder and mayhem: because it paid the bills. Rose could use any crime stories I did, and I was good at it. Did I really need the money that urgently? The literary stories might not sell—heck, might not even get published. But the satisfaction could be reward enough. It was especially on days like this, when all was so pleasant—and the stalker or psycho or whatever he was—was not in the forefront of my mind, that I gave serious thought to a different life, and yes, maybe with Elly all the time.

Breaking me out of my reverie, I heard Yves say, "This one okay?"

It was one of the larger shops on the right. We agreed it would be fine, and we breathed in the heady aroma of chocolate inside.

We were greeted by young clerks who offered us delicious samples, tiny chocolates of all different shapes, textures, and hues. Elly wanted to get small boxes of chocolates for friends in Manteo and the courthouse. She bought a slightly larger box for Mabel. I wanted to get one for Misty as a thank you for looking after my parakeet. Every time we bought anything I did a mental calculation about room in the suitcases. We were in good shape so far.

Munching on a sample, Christine came up to me. She licked chocolate off of one of her fingers, smiled big, and said, "We'll have dinner soon, so we don't eat too much chocolate . . . but I don't care."

Christine turned and joined Elly and Yves as they sauntered outside the chocolate shop to the sidewalk.

I had just reached to the tray of samples an attractive young clerk held out for me when I heard the scream from the sidewalk and then the clamoring of voices.

Turning quickly, I saw that Christine was sprawled onto the street up against the front right wheel of a white panel truck. Elly was helping her get up.

I rushed out.

Several people had gathered, all talking at once. I pushed my way up beside Yves, who helped Elly get Christine off the street. The driver of the panel truck had hopped out of the cab and rushed around too.

One of three college-age women spoke in English to anyone standing nearby, "He pushed her. Shoved her . . . bumped them with his shoulder and kept on walking."

Christine continued assuring Yves and Elly, "I'm all right. Okay. All right." She inspected the palm of her right hand. It was apparently scraped on the cobblestones when she fell. Elly and Yves stood close to Christine, still touching her. Christine flexed her shoulders, as if one might be sore.

The driver kept shaking his head and holding his hands out. I assumed he was protesting his innocence. Thankfully, the truck had been inching along by necessity because of the number of pedestrians moving very slowly. Although Christine fell into the fender of the moving truck, it did not strike her with any force.

I turned to the woman who spoke English. She had continued talking with her friends. "Where's the man who pushed her?" I said.

She looked at me. "He's gone. Right away. He didn't stop. Just shoved that woman and the other one too." She inclined her head toward Elly.

I caught my breath. "What did he look like? This man?"

"Oh, I don't know. It was all so fast. He was tall. And he wore a coat. Not a long one but . . ." She brushed her hand against her thigh. ". . . you know, not a jacket."

I came beside Elly. "You okay?" I said.

She nodded. "Fine." Then she looked at me. "He bumped both of us. Pushed us. Hard. I stumbled but didn't fall." Her face registered concern as she eyed Christine. "She's lucky . . . the truck was just creeping along."

"Did you see him? The guy who shoved you."

"No, not really. Out of the corner of my eye, maybe."

Yves, his arm around Christine's shoulders, talked with the driver of the truck, who was still apparently pleading his innocence.

I did catch enough of Yves' French to know he was not blaming the driver.

To Elly, I said, "Out of the corner of your eye, what did he . . . ?" I let my sentence drift off.

Elly knew what I wanted to know. "It could have been. Him." The impact of what had happened appeared to register. "Oh, God, it could have been," she whispered, but with an urgency in her voice. "The coat. I did see a coat. Beige. Thigh-length." She caught her breath. "It was a shove. It wasn't just bumping into me. He pushed. Hard."

I kept silent. But I put my hand on her shoulder. Reassuring.

Elly tilted her head toward Yves and Christine. "Do we tell them?"

I had thought about it just then, also. "I think we've got to."

She nodded.

"Back at the hotel. I'll tell them then," I said.

When we entered the lobby of the hotel, Yves approached one of the clerks at the desk. He came back to us with a small first aid kit the clerk had given him. He put an ointment on Christine's scuffed right palm.

"I never dropped my chocolates," Christine said with a grin. She clutched her bag of chocolates in a paper bag that was crumpled at the top.

Yves sat down with us. I said, "Yves, that might not have been an accident."

Speaking slowly and trying to enunciate clearly, I told Yves and Christine about my suspicions that I was being stalked by someone who probably wanted to do harm to me or to Elly, and how the person had followed us to Paris, we believed, and that he had also apparently followed us to Bruges.

When I was finished, Yves was silent for a minute or more. Then he said "Maybe. But nobody followed us. I would have noticed. Tomorrow, we go back a different way. More scenic. And I will be watching. We do not worry." He patted my forearm, and gave a reassuring bob to his head.

Christine chattered something in French to him, and he smiled and did that little shrug.

And that was that.

We parted and agreed to meet back in the lobby at a quarter till seven to go for dinner.

Yves had already made reservations for us at a restaurant a few blocks away near where he had parked the car.

Elly and I both took showers and changed into clothes we would probably wear tomorrow on the trip back to Paris. While she was still in the bathroom after her shower, I kicked off my shoes and stretched out on the bed and thought about what happened outside the chocolate shop. The shove against Elly, who stumbled into Christine, and how that could have been a lot worse. How in the hell did that son of a bitch follow us? How did he do it? It was bizarre and scary. Hell, it was almost supernatural.

I tried my best not to think about it. One way I avoided thinking about the bad guy was to concentrate on presenting Elly with that lovely ring. I wanted it to be at the right time and right place. Even though I had the ring with me, I didn't think there would be a suitable opportunity to do it on this quick trip to Bruges. Change that "suitable opportunity" to "a romantic enough setting."

I wanted it to be a moment Elly would always remember most dearly.

Chapter Seventeen

The four of us left the hotel and turned left to walk the four blocks or so to the restaurant where Yves had made reservations. I walked beside Yves and Christine and Elly were right behind us. Christine talked to Elly, who made appropriate brief acknowledgments.

Even as we walked, I kept my eyes alert to anything that might signal danger.

We were met in the restaurant by a smiling hostess of about forty or so. A silver necklace sparkled against the black top she wore. Yves said something to her in French and she led us to a table for four at a window near the rear. I pulled a chair out for Elly, who sat beside me; Yves was across from me, and Christine faced Elly and said something to her and chuckled. Elly tried a short laugh, also, but I'm not sure she understood what Christine had said, any more than I did.

Yves ordered a bottle of wine. When the server brought it, uncorked it, and let Yves sniff and sample and okay it with a nod of his head, Yves poured an inch or so into Elly's glass. She raised her fingers to indicate that was enough. He then poured wine for Christine and held the bottle toward my upturned glass. With a smile, I held one palm toward him and shook my head. He didn't push it. So he poured himself a nice glass. We raised our glasses—me, my water glass—and clinked them and wished good luck to us all.

The food was good. Elly got a grilled salmon and I had a pasta dish with shrimp. I'm not sure what Yves and Christine ordered. Both had a brown sauce of some kind, and they said it was quite tasty. As the French do, and as I've started imitating, we used small pieces of the bread to sop up leavings in the plate. Our plates ended up quite clean.

We got coffee at the end of the meal, and declined dessert until Christine cajoled Elly into splitting a dish of the Belgian ice cream with her. The vanilla ice cream came in a tall glass, drizzled with caramel and topped with whipped cream. The youngish man who served us, brought two long, slender spoons, smiled and went back and produced two more of the spoons. It took very little urging by Christine to get Elly to dive into the ice cream. We all sampled it, and made appreciative sounds.

While Elly and Christine were busy with the ice cream. Yves eyed me, as he had done several times during the meal, and said, "Are you all right?"

"Hmm? Oh, yes. Thanks. *Merci.*"

"You seem maybe something bother you. You still thinking about this afternoon?"

"Oh, no." I practiced my Gallic shrug. "Well, maybe a little bit."

Actually, I thought about what might be waiting for us once we were back in Paris. I had thought, too, about what Balls said concerning coming back home earlier than we had planned. That was not a bad idea. I was sure this psycho knew when we had planned to return. Plenty of our friends at the Outer Banks knew our schedule. An earlier departure might throw him off.

On the walk back to the hotel, the streets were mostly deserted. All of the young people had found other places to go rather than stroll around the streets. At one point the four of us walked abreast in the middle of one of the cobblestone streets. The polished cobblestones gave back soft glows from the tall lamps along the sidewalk, as if to share the light.

I tried to be casual about it, but I continued to glance around at our surroundings as we walked, and I eyed anyone who might appear. I knew Elly did the same thing.

At one point Yves announced that tomorrow we would head back to Paris along the coast rather than take the motor-way. "Will take longer," he said, "but more scenic."

It was something to look forward to.

In the hotel lobby we said our goodnights and agreed upon a meeting time in the morning for breakfast, look around town maybe a bit more, and start our return to Paris.

Sunshine greeted us the next morning. After breakfast in the hotel—plenty of yogurt, bread and pastries, some sliced fruit, and cheese, limply cooked bacon—we gathered our belong-ings, checked out, and Yves scurried off to bring the car around. In a few minutes I brought the two suitcases outside and stood on the sidewalk with them. Shortly, Elly and Christine joined me there in front of the hotel.

"Oh, some lace," Elly said, and she hurried across the street to a shop a woman had just opened. In no time at all, Elly was back with a big smile on her face and a small pack-age. She showed me: two picture-framed artistically ar-ranged samples of Belgium lace. "Mabel and Mother both know about the lace they make here. I know they'll like these."

In a few minutes, Yves drove up in his Peugeot, pulled partially onto the sidewalk and we stored our gear. As soon as Elly and Christine settled in, I sat in the front with Yves. Christine unfolded her map and she said something in French to Yves. He responded with a smile and shook his head. I didn't catch the exchange.

"And we're off," Yves said in English.

Not to be deterred, Christine continued to consult her map.

Yves weaved in and out of the narrow streets and shortly we were on the edge of Bruges and headed into what was mostly farmland, with occasional industrial buildings of some sort dotting the landscape. The two-lane road was well maintained. Nicely painted markings divided the highway and indicated when passing was permitted. There was virtually no other traffic.

From the backseat, Elly said, "Beautiful day for traveling. Sun and everything."

"*Oui*," Yves said.

"Thank you for making this possible, Yves and Christine," I said, and half turned in my seat to address Christine.

She looked up from her map, gave a big smile and said, "Happy to have you." She laughed and said, "I'll try not to fall in front of any more cars."

The side view mirror on my side of the car had been damaged and propped up crookedly with silver duct tape. I had to scrunch down a bit in the seat to see out of the mirror. But I did that to keep an eye on any cars that appeared to be following us. All clear for now, at any rate.

We passed through small villages where the houses and other small buildings crowded their doorways onto the narrow sidewalks, appearing almost to be toppling into the road, barely a foot or so from our car. A few times Yves took side roads in these villages to explore a bit, let us experience more of the area, savor the quaintness and a sense of the past. I could appreciate the desire of artists to want to pain these scenes, these different-hued houses—from yellow and pink, to dull gray. I thought about artists like Cezanne and Van Gogh, and how they would do it, and I wished I could paint these scenes.

We took our time and even stopped a few times. Close to lunchtime, we arrived in the town of De Haan, Belgium. Yves found a parking spot near a walkway up to the beach and the wide boardwalk there. Elly and I held hands as we went up the walkway. We got to the top at the boardwalk and saw the ocean. We looked at the ocean and then grinned at each other.

"Like back home?" Elly said.

"Sort of," I said, "if you consider the North Sea the same as the Outer Banks."

"Right now it looks like it," she said.

"Homesick?"

"No, not really, but it's always good to get back home . . . good to get away and good to get back."

I breathed in deeply. The salt air was great, and I could swear I actually smelled the health-giving properties of the ocean. "I always feel better when I see the ocean." I squeezed Elly's hand. "Not just *see* the ocean but feel it, experience it, get nourished by it."

"Me too," she said softly and brushed her shoulder tenderly against my arm.

Despite feeling good about being there at the sea, always in the back of my mind—and I couldn't help it—was the half-formed specter of that psycho lurking about. In my mind, he was not fully formed, more of a tall shadow of a man in a lightweight coat that came to his thighs. His long arms that hung down by his side.

Christine came and stood beside us. Yves walked to the beach side of the boardwalk and watched the dozens of people strolling along on the wide, sandy beach. Only one person, in a wet suit, ventured into the water. But the water did look inviting with the sun hitting it. And with only very light wind, being outside like this at the North Sea was most pleasant.

Yves left his watch post, and checked out the menu pinned on a bulletin board outside of a large restaurant on our right. He came back to us. "Mussels? Specialty of the house."

"Sounds great," I said.

We went inside and were seated and gave our orders to a fiftyish waiter in black trousers, white shirt, and black bowtie. To share, we wanted an extra large bowl of mussels; Elly and I also ordered seafood soup. A cup for her, a bowl for me.

The restaurant was filling up. Elly and I both watched the people who came in. There was a lot of chatter and laughter. Christine smiled a comment to a couple that excused themselves to squeeze past our table. I couldn't understand their French, other than to tell it was a friendly exchange. Christine turned to us. "They say the mussels are the very best in the world."

And when our waiter brought our big, steaming bowl of mussels, I figured I would agree with the couple even before I had tasted one. The mussels, their dark shells shiny with the broth, winked open at us. The broth smelled richly of butter and garlic. We had long slender forks and an extra empty bowl for the discarded shells. The waiter had also brought two baskets of bread.

While we admired the bowl of mussels—and Elly, saying she wanted to be able to show the folks back home, took a picture with her phone—our seafood soup arrived. Rich and golden, it had shrimp and fish and clams and mussels and some other little snail-like morsels I couldn't remember the name of. And it was delicious. Elly gave an appreciative tilt of her head as well when she tasted the soup.

We didn't let the soup curtail our sampling the mussels. They were perfect. Warm and moist with the broth, a tender yet slightly chewy texture. The chunks of bread went well with it all—the soup and the mussels. I dipped a piece of bread in the mussels' broth, plopped it in my mouth, and grinned at Yves, who did the same thing with a piece of bread.

In great spirits as we left the restaurant, we stood outside a few moments admiring the view of the ocean. Then Yves said, "I guess we better start on our way. We still have many kilometers to Paris." He smiled, "And other sights to see."

Settling in the car and starting out again, I think all of us were aware of how nice it would be to take a nap. So we chattered away to stay awake—and make sure Yves stayed alert.

I watched the countryside. It was hillier than the Coastal Plains back home. The ocean dropped away from high bluffs and hills instead of being approached like back home with miles of flat and then even flatter land easing into the ocean. Later in the afternoon, I saw a sign that brought to mind most vividly where we were and some of the history surrounding the area. The sign said "Dunkirk." It wasn't the English spelling we are used to, but that's what it was. That famous site in World War II where cordoned off and surrounded Allied soldiers were rescued and carried to safety aboard hundreds of small boats that came across the channel from England.

We rode along mostly in silence for quite a while. At some point we passed beyond Belgium into France. I hadn't noticed. There was no border checkpoint.

Yves glanced over at me, that half-grin playing on his face. "You want to see England?" he said.

I cocked my head at him.

"Yes," he said. He turned off the main highway on to an even narrower little road. A sign said *Nord-Pas-de-Calais.* He parked the Peugeot near four or five other cars. Several people stood on a sparsely grassed knoll looking out toward the sea.

"Come on," Yves said. We all got out and trudged behind him to the knoll. The sea spread out in front of us. "Look at the horizon," Yves said, pointing off in the distance.

Far away, along the horizon, I could see a smudgy line of washed-out white. I began to smile.

"Yes," Yves said. "The White Cliffs of Dover . . . England."

Elly stood close beside me. "Unbelievable," she said. "Here we are in France looking at England."

When we left the knoll, the afternoon was definitely waning. We rarely spoke as we restarted our drive. Shortly the few cars we met had their lights on. Night was definitely on its way. The miles clicked away. Before long I could see the headlights of the Peugeot brushing along the road.

About thirty minutes later, Yves raised one hand off the steering wheel to point toward the horizon. "That glow," he said, "is Paris."

I sensed that Elly leaned forward, the same as I had. The glow took up at least half of the horizon. "The City of Light," I muttered. I felt good. Like a sense of coming home.

"In a few minutes," Yves said, "we'll actually be able to see the whole city."

He was right. Not ten minutes later we crested a long hill and Yves, checking his rearview mirror, signaled he was pulling off the road and parking. He engaged his hazard lights. We coasted to a stop.

There, laid out in all of its splendor, was the faraway City of Paris. The lights stretched across the entire horizon. We couldn't see individual lights, but taken together the illumination became a blanket of light that warmed the land and the sky.

"Beautiful," Elly breathed. She had her hands on the backs of the front seats.

Again, that sense of coming home. Paris had done that to me. A second home, so to speak, and it had felt that way since my college days, even before I had made the first trip. Reading about Hemingway and all of the other writers and artists who had come to the city after World War I, Paris became my city as well. It was as if, yes, I had lived here too, some time in another life.

But now, right now, there was a darkness clouding my feeling of the city. That stalker was not giving up. And I sensed that he was getting bolder, closer to a turning point when he would do something. What, I wasn't sure. Just that sense of dread that enveloped me.

Best to throw him off. That settled it. My mind was made up. Following Balls' suggestion, we would leave earlier than planned. Get back home.

I would get on the ticketing tomorrow morning. With

luck we should be able to fly back by Friday.

Yves glanced over at me, a smile on his lips. But the smile faded as he looked at me. I lowered my head, and stared at my folded hands.

"You okay?" Yves asked.

"Fine," I said. "Just fine."

But I knew I wasn't. I knew it was not all over. Not by a long shot.

Chapter Eighteen

Yves eased onto the road and we began the final leg of the ride back to Paris. Christine had folded her map and she tapped me lightly with it and pointed at the glove compartment. I stowed it away.

"What a wonderful trip you have made for us," Elly said. She looked first at Christine and then leaned forward and touched Yves on the shoulder. "I mean it," she said. "This has been a once in a lifetime experience . . . a real adventure."

"It has been fun," Christine said. "So good to be with you." Christine chuckled. "It is good to see you smile so much. You smile a lot."

I was determined to smile also.

Paris began with the industrial buildings, miles away from the center of the city. We passed under an overhead directional sign for Charles De Gaulle Airport. Yes, getting closer. And the traffic was building up. I checked the time. Close to eight o'clock. There was slightly more vehicular traffic on the outbound road than on our side heading into the center city. We passed the multi-lane loop road around the city and began weaving among various roads that Yves was obviously familiar with. At one point he flipped his thumb to the left and we saw the brilliantly lighted Opera, in all its glory, squatting there between outstretched streets and overlooking an expanse of concrete and cobblestone.

We took one of the lower bridges across the Seine. To our right the Eiffel Tower blinked on its lights, dominating the skyline.

Elly breathed out sighs of appreciation.

"No place like it in the world," I said, and Elly reached across and squeezed my shoulder. She didn't have to say anything. We knew how fortunate we were. I rehearsed in my mind how in the world I could thank Yves and Christine sufficiently for this trip. It seemed like anything I could say would fall short of what I felt.

After we crossed the bridge, Yves began to make his way to the left, and we were truly heading home.

He maneuvered onto Blvd. St. Germain, past the 1920s Hemingway haunt of Aux Deux Magots to Place Maubert, and took the little one-way street to our Rue des Grands Degres. He was able to stop in front of the apartment with no one behind us. We got out and popped the trunk for our luggage. Christine, as usual, had literally hopped out of the car, scurried around to give Elly and me big hugs. I gave Yves a hug also; not just a pass at a man-type hug, but a real hug. We stood there a few moments thanking them. A small delivery truck came up behind us and the driver waited for us to say our final goodbyes and Yves and Christine got back in the car, waving goodbye, and Elly and I went into the apartment building. She carried her gift packages and I carried our suitcase.

We flipped on lights as soon as we entered the apartment. Everything looked good. I put the suitcase on the bed.

"I guess we should eat something," I said. "Not really hungry, but . . ."

"Soup and baguette suits me," Elly said. "Maybe some fruit." She opened the refrigerator and peered inside. "If we are going to leave—leave earlier than Sunday—we'd better start getting rid of some of this food."

While Elly was busy elsewhere, I secreted the ring deep inside a drawer with my clothes. Maybe there would be a time and place tomorrow night to present her the ring. I chuckled to myself. It was getting to be a real project, finding the proper opportunity.

After we ate, I said I could start the whole business of switching our airline tickets, but I decided to wait until first thing in the morning. Just didn't feel up to dealing with the airlines tonight.

"I'm going to take a shower," Elly said, "and put my pajamas on."

"Yes, me too," I said. "Seems like it's been a long day."

Thursday morning I'd start in on the tickets after we'd had breakfast down the street. The little café at the corner to our left, where our street ended at rue Maitre Albert, served a customary light breakfast that most of the places did—a fresh croissant, jelly, yogurt, and freshly squeezed orange juice from the little machine that sat at the rear of the counter, and coffee of course. That was plenty. It was warm enough we sat outside at the sidewalk.

Elly inclined her head toward the musical toyshop to our right, the *Avanti la Musica.* "She opens in the afternoon," Elly said. "I want to get something there to take to Martin. A real nice toy, not just something to play with in the sand, but something he will keep." She smiled at me. "And something I will enjoy, too . . . like a music box." The woman's husband made some of the music boxes and they ordered others from Germany. A fascinating little store, chock full of the music boxes, marionettes and unique toys. I thought of it as more of a toyshop for people our age than for children.

When we finished, we sat there a few more minutes, watching cars come by and delivery trucks that had to maneuver carefully, sometimes backing up and making a couple of passes, to navigate the sharp and narrow turn onto rue Maitre Albert. A middle-aged couple entered the café and we exchanged *bonjours.* Even though we studiously avoiding saying anything about it, both of us kept alert for the Evil One. Part of our seemingly casual people-watching was directed at keeping an eye out for any disturbing surfacing of that character.

Finally, I signaled the young woman who served us and

settled the bill with her. I paid in euros instead of credit card. I needed to get rid of any surplus euros, just saving back enough for taxi to the airport and a few tips perhaps.

"Okay," I said, "time to tackle the airlines, change our tickets."

"There'll be a penalty?"

"Oh, yes," I said. "The airlines will get their pound of flesh . . . and more."

Actually, when I buckled down to it in the apartment and called the airlines, it wasn't as painful as I thought it would be. We secured a flight out in the morning, leaving Charles De Gaulle at nine-thirty-five nonstop to Newark and then a two-and-a-half layover for a flight down to Norfolk. The layover was good. Plenty of time to go through customs and recheck our luggage. Still by the end of the day it would be a long one, and by the time we drove from Norfolk to the Outer Banks it would be eight or nine o'clock at night.

"Tonight, let's have a nice dinner at the Smoking Goose."

Elly agreed. "I'm sad to be leaving. Aren't you?"

"I'm always sad to leave Paris," I said. "But, let's think about how nice it will be to get back home."

Tonight would be the night to present the ring. Either at dinner, if it was quiet and private enough, or back here at the apartment when we return. I was looking forward to it. Elly would love the ring. But I was sure neither of us fully realized what the ring would represent. I continued to wrestle with it. Certainly a commitment. An engagement? Marriage? I believed the thought of marriage frightened both of us. And I wasn't sure if that never-really-expressed apprehension was enough to make us avoid taking that ultimate step.

But we were definitely getting closer, and maybe this ring would be the catalyst that moved the inevitable forward.

By early afternoon, we had put out clothes we would wear tomorrow on the flight and most of the packing was done, or at least it was arranged so we could finish quite quickly in the morning.

Elly came into the living room where I was checking emails on my computer. "The musical toyshop should be open by now," she said.

I clicked off the computer. "I'll walk down there with you, and then go check out with Francois Madet," I said, referring to the real-estate owner with whom we dealt.

Elly didn't object to my walking down the block with her. We didn't say anything about it, but both of us scanned the street and sidewalks. Impossible not to think about that person being here in Paris.

Sarah, the petite owner of the toyshop, brushed back a lock of her brown hair and greeted us with a smile. Another couple came in behind us. Sarah had obviously just opened the shop and she scurried about turning on additional lights and starting a twinkling piped-in music.

To Elly I said, "Stay here until I get back. Shouldn't take me but a few minutes."

Elly nodded and picked up one of the music boxes.

I hurried back up our street past the apartment to the intersection and turned left to Madet's office. Madet greeted me and I explained about leaving tomorrow instead of Sunday and he said no problem and to leave the keys on the kitchen counter, the apartment unlocked because the cleaning lady would come that afternoon.

Everything was falling into place.

I felt good as I left Madet's and started back to the musical toyshop.

It was then that my cell phone rang.

Chapter Nineteen

I stopped in midstride there on the sidewalk and frowned at my cell phone. I didn't recognize the number. I answered, a bit of caution in my tone.

The voice was breathless as though the caller were walking rapidly while trying to talk. "There's a killing . . ." a man said. It was a Southern US accent, but a cultured voice. ". . . there on Pont L'Archeveche."

The caller disconnected.

Pont L'Archeveche was the bridge up two short blocks and across the quay from the Smoking Goose restaurant—and only a little more than a block from the musical toyshop, where Elly was. Or at least that's where she was when I left her.

A heavy sense of dread enveloped me. Just like that. Feeling good one moment and then steeped in a dark, pressing, hard-to-breathe foreboding. As if in a daze, I jammed the cell phone into my pocket. I had to make sure Elly was still safely at the toyshop. But I had to investigate. There was absolutely no way I couldn't. The caller had to be the psycho. Had to be. Then I energized myself; I squared my shoulders. This might be it.

Almost at a jog, I hurried back to the musical toyshop.

Elly wasn't there.

"Oh, my God. Where?" I stepped farther into the store.

Sarah was at the back with two customers.

She saw me and apparently saw the expression on my face, and she gave the slightest shrug to let me know she didn't know where Elly was.

Three other shoppers browsed around marveling at the displays, and playing a music box from time to time. I heard tinkling variations of "La Vie En Rose" competing with one another.

Where the hell was Elly?

Jesus, not the bridge.

I ran toward the bridge, dodging others on the sidewalk. I got a few stares.

I had gone just a block when I heard the "ooo-eee, ooo-eee" of police sirens. It was a different sound over here than at home. Emergency vehicles sounded more like they did in the movies.

Watching for a non-fatal break in the traffic—or the stoplight, whichever came first—I stood in front of the Smoking Goose, casting my eyes around at the people. Across the street, a crowd was beginning to converge a few yards onto the bridge, Pont L'Archveche. The traffic light gave me a break and I dashed across the boulevard just as a police car came from the right. The police cruiser's tires squealed turning onto the bridge. It screeched to a halt. Two officers jumped out and hurried to the group of people who gawked at something lying on the sidewalk.

Another police car; then another.

Uniformed officers gave harsh sounding commands to the dozen or more people who had gathered, forcing them to back away.

My heart stopped. I'm convinced of it.

There, lying on the sidewalk was a young woman.

Oh, thank God. It was not Elly.

The young woman was sprawled on her side, her face close to the concrete balustrade, and there was fresh blood— very red—pooling around her back. It appeared she bled from two or three wounds in her back. Stabbed? Gunshot? Couldn't tell. One of the officers knelt and checked quickly for a pulse. In a moment, he looked up at one of the other officers and shook his head.

CALLING CARDS OF DEATH

Three young women, who looked about the same age as the woman lying on the pavement, wouldn't back away. They stood there, their eyes wide. Two of the three were sobbing openly. The third one hugged her arms tightly about her body as she tried to answer something an officer was asking her. She trembled as she forced the words out.

More people tried to gather. The officers made them stay back. Another police vehicle pulled up. Traffic was virtually halted on the boulevard. The bridge was closed off.

I managed to stand as close as I could, staying in the forefront. I had to step back as yellow crime tape was secured.

Two obviously medical tech types approached from an ambulance that had forced its way onto the bridge; they knelt beside the body, checked again for pulse, then stood and spoke to the officer closest to them. They spoke French, of course, and I could only catch a word every now and then.

I concentrated on the scene but at the same time cast my sight around at the people who crowded as close as the officers would permit. I scanned the faces of the people. Did I really expect to see that son of a bitch? And with a chill, I was sure he was the one who had done this, who had killed this young woman.

One of the medical techs spoke again to the officer standing closest to him, the one who appeared to be in charge. The officer nodded and the tech rolled the woman over partially so he could see the front of the body. There was no blood. He rolled her back to her side. The tech looked up at the officer and made a motion with his right hand, a movement as if he used a knife to stab. The tech stepped away and one of the officers began taking pictures.

I shifted my position slightly so I would be closer to where the three women stood. They had to be friends of the victim. A foursome of young college-age women on vacation, enjoying the sights and the lovely weather, and then this.

An officer spoke to the woman who hugged her body, arms tight, as if trying to prevent herself from trembling. She said something in English, and the officer motioned for another officer, an older one whose girth had probably increased with age. He spoke English to the woman. I couldn't hear everything they said. But enough of it. She told him they had just stopped on the bridge to watch the tour boats and look at the river, and she said "Canada," and I assumed that was where they were from.

The older officer wrote something in a notepad he held. Names and where they were staying, next of kin, that sort of thing I was sure. While he jotted down information, a plainclothes officer approached. He glanced at the body, nodded to the medical techs and they covered the victim with a beige blanket. Other officers continued to work keeping the crowd back.

The plainclothes officer looked more like a graduate student than a detective. He wore a tie with his dark suit. He was trim and his hair was cut neatly. When he came to the older officer, the officer said what sounded like "Yes, sir," or the equivalent. The detective nodded and then spoke to the woman in English. She said something along the lines of "no idea," "didn't see it happen . . . didn't know anything until I saw her collapse."

I wrestled with whether I needed to step forward and speak to the young detective . . . and tell him what? I didn't know for sure the psycho had done this, although I was sure he had. Tell him that I had been stalked by someone from America and not exactly threatened but figured I was being threatened and maybe Elly too, and that this was another way of letting us know he was on our trail. My thoughts drifted off. Even playing it through my mind, trying to explain my suspicions sounded, even to me, too implausible to believe. Not accomplishing anything. Nonetheless, part of me wanted to speak up. My civic duty? Would it really add anything? Or just muddy the waters even more?

Earlier, I had noticed a couple of items lying near the woman's body, but I hadn't paid too much attention to the items. Instead, I had concentrated on the body lying there in pool of blood. Then, however, the detective said something to the woman he interviewed, and she pointed to a small dark-colored backpack lying beside the shrouded body. She indicated with a motion of her hand that the victim was carrying the backpack by one of its straps, not wearing it.

Another item lay near the backpack.

The young woman shook her head and said, "It's not hers."

She had pointed to a beret. A black beret with a silver replica of the Eiffel Tower affixed to the edge of it.

I sucked in my breath.

Exactly like the beret Elly had bought in the Lain Quarter.

Hell, that psycho must have thrown it down.

Another calling card.

And I thought about Elly. Where the hell was she?

The killer was out there.

I had to get back to find Elly. Keep her safe.

Chapter Twenty

I repeatedly mumbled "*pardon*" as I pushed away from the crime scene through the throng of people who hung there despite repeated call by the police to keep back.

Vehicular traffic had come to almost a standstill on the boulevard. Without waiting for the light, I weaved in and out among the cars and dashed across to the Smoking Goose and did a modified jog/fast walk to the musical toyshop.

I exhaled a breath of relief.

Elly and shop-owner Sarah stood at the front door of the store, peering up toward the bridge and all of the activity there. They saw me hurrying up. Elly stared at me, obviously trying to read my face, and I was reading hers too. Deep concern etched there in both of our faces. And maybe something else in her face.

I spoke much more harshly than I intended. "Where were you? I stopped here and you weren't . . ."

"I went next door to get Martin a set of colored pencils from the art store. Sarah was busy, and . . . What's going on?"

Sarah spoke to me, her English heavily accented. "Woman up there killed? That's what the people say."

I nodded, my eyes on Elly. "Stabbed," I said. Elly wrapped her arms around her body, much as did the young woman on the bridge. A comforting thing? To keep from shivering?

"Let's go back to the apartment," I said to Elly. Then I added quickly: "You get what you needed?"

"Yes." Her voice was weak. She seemed frozen in place.

"Let's go then," I said again.

"Was it him?" she said. She hadn't moved.

"I think so," I said.

She glanced around, as if looking to make sure no one approached. Then I knew what the expression was that I saw in her eyes. It was fear. She gave a quick shudder and then appeared to control herself. Chin thrust bravely forward, she said, "He was here, Harrison. He was here."

"*What?*" I almost shouted. I looked around and then back at Elly.

"He was here. There were several people in the store. Tourists. Most of them speaking English, so when he said something I didn't know at first he was talking to me. His voice behind me. He said, 'It's not over.' It was an American voice. Southern but not real Southern."

I took one of her hands. It was cold. In her other hand, she clutched a white paper bag that I knew held her purchases for her son Martin and maybe others.

"When I realized he was talking to me I turned around, but he had left or was leaving. There was a man leaving, his back to me. He was tall and wore a beige windbreaker jacket. A long one, and he disappeared out of the store. Along with other people."

I squeezed her hand. "You didn't get a good look at him?"

She shook her head. "It was fast, and he was gone." She touched her lips with the fist of her hand that held her purchases. "As I said, at first I didn't think he was talking to me . . ." Her voice trailed off.

Sarah had stepped out a yard or so beyond the sidewalk to get a better view of what was going on at the bridge. "Very bad," she muttered. "Very bad."

"To the apartment," I said to Elly.

She nodded as if she acquiesced, even though I wasn't at all sure she knew what I said.

I kept hold of her hand as we walked steadily back to the

apartment. While glancing from time to time at Elly's face, I kept casting my eyes about for anyone else on the street or sidewalk. Elly stared straight ahead.

As we got to the big door for the apartment building, I said, "Is that all that he said? 'It's not over.'"

"That was it." She shook her head. "I just wish I'd looked at him right away." She squeezed my hand. "But I didn't even think he was talking to . . ." She started repeating that statement but let it die.

"I understand," I said, and I punched in the code for our building. When we went in the main door, I made sure the iron grate was closed and locked while we waited for the little elevator to arrive, which it did in a few seconds. We stood close together in the elevator. Heck, you had to.

She looked up at my face. "You really think he killed the woman on the bridge?"

"I'm virtually certain of it." Now was not the time to hold anything back, so I told her about the beret that lay beside the body. The beret that did not belong to the victim. "It was exactly the same type, same design, that you bought," I said.

The elevator creaked to a stop at our floor. As I unlocked the door to our apartment, Elly said, "How did you know? When you first went to the bridge? You knew something then."

"Telephone," I said. "He called on my cell." I locked the door behind us as we stepped inside. "His almost exact words were, 'There's a killing on Pont L'Archeveche.' He didn't say he'd killed her. I remember that."

"But he did . . ." she said, her voice sounding stronger but still trailing off at the end of her sentence.

"I'm sure of it." We moved toward the kitchen and living room. "And he threw down that beret—another of his calling cards. May have tossed the knife in the Seine and then kept on walking. He was walking when he called me. Walking real fast. I could tell by the way he was breathing."

Setting down her bags from the stores, Elly stood leaning against the kitchen counter. "Did you tell the police? Tell them anything about, well, like maybe you knew . . . but how could you? You don't know who he is. What could you really tell them?"

I stood beside her, rubbing my hands together as if they were cold. "I thought about the same thing. That maybe I should say something. But what? I'm still not sure whether I did the right thing by not saying anything."

Elly got two glasses out of the cabinet. "Water?"

I nodded and kept looking at my hands.

She opened the refrigerator for the water.

We both drank. Still holding her half-empty glass, Elly said, "I want to go home."

"Yes, I know the feeling," I said. "Well, tomorrow morning." I set my empty glass down. "Leave this son of a bitch behind us."

"I hope so," she said.

I moved to the house phone. "I'm going to call Balls. Bring him up to date on the latest." Punching in the numbers, I waited a few seconds to the clicking sounds connecting to the other end. Mid-morning back home. After a couple of rings, Balls answered, not sounding as gruff as usual.

"I thought it might be you," he said.

"We've got something else," I said, and I told him about the cell phone call and the slain young woman on the bridge, and I told him about what was said to Elly in the toyshop. He listened until I took a breath and stopped.

Then he said, "Did you talk to the police?"

"No, I didn't. I was not sure I should . . . or what to tell them."

"Wouldn't have done much good. Just get you tangled up in it. Delay your departure. You coming home?"

"Yes, tomorrow. Morning. Be there late in the day. Night."

"Don't spread the word around that you're leaving. Surprise that bastard."

He was silent for a moment. Then he said, "Keep an eye on Ms. Pedersen." He referred to Elly. "He may try to get to you through her."

I glanced over at Elly. I thought she could hear what Balls was saying, but her face was inscrutable, like she was determined to be brave. "Yes, I've thought about that. The beret and all."

Another pause. "Don't worry about the police. I've been talking with a detective friend over there. Met him at the FBI academy. He's checked on you and Ms. Pedersen a couple of times."

"I haven't seen him."

"You wouldn't. He's good. And he hasn't been what you'd call a constant presence. So he's stayed outta the way. I'll fill him in . . . after you're on your way."

"Thanks, Balls. We'll be glad to get home."

"What time is it over there?"

I glanced at my watch. "A little after four," I said.

"Stay in tonight. Don't go wandering around."

"Yes, we'll be staying in the apartment," I said. "And all locked up."

When we disconnected, I studied Elly's face. I gave a half-hearted shrug. "So much for our farewell dinner tonight at the Smoking Goose."

"I don't want to go anywhere," she said. She tried for a lighter approach. "Besides, we'll need to go to bed early so we can get up early." She picked up her package from the toyshop. "Besides, there's still a little packing."

"I'll arrange for a cab at six-thirty. Be at the airport two hours before our flight."

I unlocked the apartment door, stepped out in the hall and summoned the elevator and relocked the apartment while I waited for the creaking arrival. Salaam, the night clerk for the tiny hotel next door had just come on duty; I asked him to call us a cab for six-thirty in the morning.

Speaking French, he could deal with the taxi dispatcher better than I could. I insisted he take a five euro note for his service.

Outside of the hotel, I looked both ways up and down our little street. Except for an elderly couple at the far end of the street, it was empty. That would be an excellent way for Balls' detective friend to observe and not be noticed himself. Have his wife or friend with him, like a mature couple taking a stroll. I went back into our apartment building.

Since we would be staying in, so much for presenting the ring to Elly tonight at the Smoking Goose.

Oh, well, while it would have been nice to give her the ring here in Paris, there would certainly be good times back home. Surely.

Chapter Twenty-One

After we had eaten a light supper from the food leftover in the refrigerator, Elly glanced at the clock and said she would call home, alert her mother that she would call again when we landed in Newark.

As she dialed, Elly said to me, "It's only a little after one in the afternoon there." Her mother answered and Elly told her we'd be leaving early in the morning. She said, "But it'll be nine or after tomorrow night before we get to the Outer Banks."

She listened for a moment or two. I could hear Mrs. Pedersen's voice on the line but not well enough to make out what she was saying.

"Yes, yes," Elly said. "I'll call from Newark and from Norfolk, too. But if it's late when we get to Norfolk, I may just spend the night at Harrison's rather than come home close to ten o'clock."

Before she signed off, Elly agreed to give a short ring when we got to my house, and that she would come home early Saturday morning. Martin would not be in school, and she could hardly wait to see him. "Yes, I love you too," she said.

We went to bed. I doubt if either of us slept soundly. Both of us waked fully before the alarm went off at five-thirty. A bit of travel anxiety, among other anxieties.

Elly started the coffee while I took a quick shower. Then it was her turn. We kept passing each other in the bedroom, kitchen, back and forth. We talked very little, just concentrated on getting last minute stuff together. By six-ten I was almost ready to take the suitcases downstairs. We did a few more last minute checks before heading downstairs.

I opened the iron gate and then the main heavy wooden outside door and started getting the suitcases out on the sidewalk. Five minutes before the taxi should arrive. The street was empty and quiet. I remembered how in Washington there was so much activity, even at six-thirty in the morning; and here, it was relatively still until eight or even later. Even though the street was bare, I kept looking around. Wanted to make sure. Checked my watch. Time for the taxi. With two minutes to spare, a Mercedes sedan taxi pulled up, the red light on the roof illuminated.

The driver got out as the trunk popped open. With a smile, he said, *"Bonjour."* He began helping me get the suit-cases into the trunk. He was maybe forty years old; dark skinned, probably from India or that part of the world. He spoke English with a heavy accent, not a French accent, I didn't think.

Elly and I kept the carry-on and laptop, along with a small cloth briefcase of mine, in the backseat with us. I keep money and other valuables in the briefcase and I make sure it stays with me at all times while traveling. I keep my passport in a pouch around my neck. Elly keeps hers quite handy in her small purse she wears close to her breast.

The driver looked back at us with a smile and said, "Charles De Gaulle Airport? Correct?"

"Yes." I knew that later he would want to know the air-line and which terminal the plane would be leaving from.

Elly sat close to me. She looked back over her shoulder as the cab pulled away. "Goodbye, little apartment," she said. "We'll miss you."

"Yes, we will," I said and squeezed her hand.

We were in for what I knew would be a trip of forty-five minutes, maybe even an hour, depending on traffic. Much of the traffic, however, would be coming into Paris, not leaving the city as we were doing.

And leaving Paris always makes me rather sad.

Of course this trip was overlain with the oppressive weight of that psycho being here also. So it was not like other visits and departures. I thought about that, and I looked at Elly and said, "We've got to come back, when all of this other business with . . . with you know who and what . . . when all of it is over. I don't want to leave Paris with a lasting impression of . . . of fleeing."

"We're not *fleeing*," she said. "Well, maybe sort of." She tried a smile at me and patted my wrist. "And, yes, we'll come back to your Paris."

I returned her smile. "It now belongs to both of us."

Once the driver had gotten through the center of the city and was on one of the main highways toward the airport, he turned his head slightly toward us and said, "Did you enjoy Paris?"

"Oh, yes," Elly said.

"Always," I said.

Then he wanted to know where we were from and did we plan to come back to Paris, and he told us where he was from (and I was right) but that he had been in Paris for fifteen years and he was not a "newcomer."

When we began to see the overhead signs giving directions to Charles De Gaulle, he asked about our airline and which terminal. I checked the tickets again. I told him the airline and terminal two.

The traffic was heavy there at the airport. Very heavy. And so early in the morning, too. People with piles of suitcases were everywhere. We secured a cart for our bags and the driver helped us as quickly as he could because he knew he had to move his car. He kept glancing around to make sure he wasn't getting blocked in by those double-parking. I had paid him and given him a fairly reasonable tip, and he thanked me and got in his car, peering out his window at approaching traffic and squeezed out into an exit lane.

I pushed our cart and Elly kept my brief case in one

hand and her oversize purse in the other. We checked in with a cheerful young woman at the counter and our bags were on their way. With boarding passes in hand, we headed toward security. The crowds were so dense the whole experience took on a surreal aura, like we were in a fluid river of humanity, being swept along with everyone else.

It wasn't long before we had cleared the hurdles of passport control and security and took seats side-by-side at the gate to await the boarding process.

Trying not to be too obvious about it, I scanned the crowds of people. Not really expecting anything but the way this character had shown up as if by magic kept me constantly looking.

Boarding went orderly and we got our nice seats in business class, a real treat for us. Big new airplane. A Boeing 777. The triple-seven. Just like on the trip over, Elly grinned about her seat and the different positions it could be put into by pushing the buttons. We settled in. The flight attendants were most attentive and offered us coffee or other beverages.

With the engines idling and rocking the aircraft gently there on the tarmac, it is always sleep-inducing for me. My eyes felt heavy. So I got out a notepad and pen, ready to do some serious thinking once we were airborne. Elly said she would try to watch another movie on the good size screen in front of her. I kept a casual eye on the map with the icon of a plane that would make its way from France, across the southern tip of England, Ireland, and out into the North Atlantic toward Iceland off to the right and then Canada a long, long way off. I was always curious about how cold it was a few feet away outside the aluminum skin of the aircraft at thirty-seven thousand feet, and what was our ground speed, and whether we had a tailwind or headwind, and usually a headwind going west-northwest as we would be heading. What I could do with this information was absolutely nothing, of course. But it was fun to know.

We began the full-power roar down the runway, the

force of which pressed us back in our seats. Elly put a hand on my arm, applied a bit of pressure. She whispered, "And we're off."

Gaining altitude, we made a gentle swing to the left. I enjoyed looking out the window and watching the earth slip away. As we neared cruising altitude, I put my notepad on the tray, determined to write down characteristics that I knew this psycho had to have. Maybe by listing them, I figured, perhaps—just perhaps—I could get some sort of idea of who he might be.

And a man, yes. No way this could be a woman.

So the first thing I wrote down was "man."

Elly looked at me. She knew what I was preparing to do. She nodded and put her headset on, keyed up a movie. She mouthed, "Good luck."

And I began my list.

Chapter Twenty-Two

Okay, how old was this psycho? I'd say forty maximum. Why? The few words I'd heard and that Elly had heard would peg him as not old, and certainly not a kid.. And, too, if he was someone I'd met some years ago—and the evidence was that he had known me for a number of years, at least to back when I smoked Kool cigarettes—he might be close to forty but not older than that.

So if he had known me or certainly knew who I was, it was obvious that I'd had contact with him in the past. Where? When? I'd held a number of writing seminars. Could he have been in one of those classes? And did I offend him in some way? Or, in writing about true crime, was he related to someone I wrote about, some criminal type? And now he wanted to get revenge for what I wrote?

Both of these were distinct possibilities: a former adult writing student or a person emotionally and maybe physically close to a criminal I wrote about. In the writing classes—and some were on fiction as well as nonfiction—I was always careful not to put anyone down about their writing. I made sure I didn't destroy anyone's dreams. However, especially in fiction, I know how personal the writing can be and even the tiniest bit of criticism can sometimes have devastating effect. I'm aware of that.

Some of the true crime articles I've written could get dicey. The only times I was threatened during the fact-gathering phase was when I had a camera with me. The persons connected in some way with the research I was doing never seemed to mind that I scribbled down notes on a small pad.

But a camera was another thing.

I glanced up from my notepad a moment, the hint of a wry smile tugging at my lips, remembering when the two Neuchok brothers from New Jersey had threatened to "break me in half" if I tried to take a picture of where their murdered sister had worked. And they were tough enough they could easily have fulfilled their promise. That day I had excused myself and backed off. But early the next morning before anyone was up, I drove back to the scene, got out of the car, rushed up close, took the picture, and scrambled away—safely. Without being broken in half.

There were a couple of other times, too, when the sight of a camera caused a flare-up. But none of these incidents, or any others that I could think of, would suggest the long simmering hatred, the psychological obsession that this person had for me. From what I'd read about psychos, those who become obsessed with another individual based that fixation on various things, and one of the most common was a psychotic sense that the individual being stalked had somehow gained a degree of fame or adulation that the psycho felt should be his. Another trigger could be that the psycho believed that the individual had unjustly criticized him or ridiculed him in some way. Made light of him.

It wasn't long before the flight attendants began to get ready to serve lunch. I glanced at my watch. Yes, I guessed it was getting close to that time. Or was it brunch? Didn't make any difference. I was ready for a bit of diversion. Elly concentrated on a movie. Occasionally she chuckled over something on the screen. I was happy to see her relaxing enough to enjoy the movie.

Before the meal was served—whichever meal it was—I pondered more about the psycho. A couple of things were obvious: He didn't work, not at a regular job with set hours, one that didn't permit him the time to take off and track me around; and, too, he had to be well off financially. He could pick up and fly over to Paris. I tried to think back about any

former adult students I'd had and whether they were loaded
with money. No one came to mind. Nor did I remember anyone connected with a crime story who was wealthy, although
there could have been. Same with the students. I didn't know
them all that well. Any one of them could have had a dollar-
rich nest egg, and I wouldn't necessarily have been aware of
it.

A few vaguely familiar faces came to mind when I tried
diligently to reconstruct mentally what some of the writing
classes had looked like. I could visualize people sitting
around a table and one or two of them were recognizable to
me now from a few years past. I remembered JoAnn
something who, as a result of the class on nonfiction, got a
job with the local newspaper. But that was about as good as I
could do.

The male flight attendant approached with food. I put
away my notepad to make room for the tray. With a smile,
he wanted to know what I might like to drink. Elly was being
served by a female flight attendant, who poured Elly a glass
of tomato juice. The juice with ice looked good and that's
what I ordered too.

Contrary to what many people opine, I enjoy airline
food, if for no other reason than the surprise of not knowing
what you are going to get. Elly and I ate.

Her movie was about over. When it ended, and the flight
attendants had taken away our trays, Elly nodded toward the
seat pocket where I had stowed my notepad. "Any luck?" she
said.

I shrugged. "Not more than we already have surmised,"
I said. "Male, not more than forty, probably younger by five
or more years. More than likely independently well off financially. Not working at a regular job. So has the freedom
to move around freely."

I studied her face as I continued, leaning in close to her.
"Possibly he was connected in some fashion with one of the
crime stories, but more likely I met him, or he met me, in

one of the writing classes I taught."

Thinking about what I had just said, I added, "Probably in one of the writing classes because that's when someone would have noticed I was smoking Kool cigarettes. I don't think in doing one of the crime stories there would have been occasion for much connection with personal habits, like what brand of cigarettes I smoked . . . and certainly not with the Hemingway short stories."

Elly nodded. "Makes sense." Then, "But nobody comes to mind?"

"No," I said. "Not at all. Oh, vaguely I remember some of the people but not vividly. No one stands out. In a couple of the classes—or seminars that lasted a few evenings—there were fifteen or more people. Especially in fiction writing. The short story." I gave a humorless chuckle. "I remember there were some real characters in the fiction classes. One or two had their own theories about fiction writing and—while not confrontational—certainly had ideas of their own."

"One of them, maybe?" she said.

"I don't know." I shook my head the tiniest bit. "I really don't know." Then it occurred to me. I knew it was a long shot and the chances were it would not spark any revelations, but I did have stored away in an old file in the utility room notes from some of the classes. I might have a roster or two giving students' names. Perhaps perusing those rosters—if there were any left—might get memory juices flowing. Worth a shot.

Checking the video map, I noted we were at thirty-seven thousand feet, with a ground speed of five hundred fifty-four miles an hour and the temperature outside the aircraft was a minus fifty-seven. Rather chilly if you were riding the wing.

Time to read a bit, then maybe snooze. Glancing at Elly, I saw she was engrossed in another movie. But I did think her eyes fluttered from time to time. Maybe naptime for her, too, before long.

I was reading a novel by Phil Bowie, *Killing Ground*,

centering on efforts by a group of vigilantes to thwart elephant poaching in Africa. Phil, a friend from New Bern, North Carolina, an excellent writer, makes Africa and the exciting action come vividly alive. I quickly became involved in the narrative. Time slipped by.

Elly returned from a trip forward to the restroom, and took her seat beside me. She smiled weakly. "Long flight," she said.

"Yes, about eight hours going west. With a tailwind, about seven going over."

"More than three thousand miles," she said. Another more genuine smile. "Quite a bit farther than from Manteo to Nags Head or Kill Devil Hills, which is the usual extent of my traveling." She reached over and patted my wrist. "Thank you, Harrison."

I felt a real rush of affection for her. I guess that's love. Funny how it sweeps over you from time to time when you least expect it, triggered by who knows what—a smile, a facial expression, or as the song says, just by studying the small things the other person does constantly, the tiny habits or idiosyncrasies that are so much a part of the other person. The way they lightly chew their lower lip. Or touch a lock of hair. Or how they frequently rub the ball of the thumb against the index finger while pondering something. Thousands of little things.

Later when I checked the video map, we were approaching north of Maine. Wouldn't be long now before we'd be over Boston and then toward New York/Newark. Elly saw me looking at the map and she gave a thumbs-up. "Getting closer," she mouthed.

After a period of time, we began a gentle descent that I could feel, and I checked the map for confirmation. Approach to the airport was steady with only a bit of bumpy air through low clouds; then bright afternoon sunshine as we came in toward our designated runway. I watched the ground coming up. We touched down and the captain reversed the thrust on the engines, applied a heavy foot on the brakes, and we began a seatbelt-straining slowdown; then more sedate taxiing. "Back in the US of A," Elly said. "It's hard to believe that just a few hours ago we were in Paris . . . and now here."

"Leg number one," I said. "Still a ways to go."

After the routine of exiting and going through, passport control, customs, rechecking bags, and the other hurdles, we made our way to Terminal 2 for our layover of two hours.

As promised, Elly called her mother, using my cell phone, which I had fully charged on the plane from Paris. "Yes," she said at one point, "I'll call again from Norfolk . . . and from Harrison's, if you're still awake." A pause. Then, "Yes, Mother, I'll call anyway. Don't get Martin too excited. I'll see him in the morning and surprise him. I'll be happy to see him . . . and you, too, of course."

When she finished the call, and gave me back my phone, we just sat there quietly. At that point, I think we had both morphed into a sort of catatonic state, numbed out, staring off into the distance. After a while, Elly said, "I've got to get up and take a walk and look around. Do you want something to drink? Coffee?"

"No, thanks," I said. "Don't get lost."

"I'll leave a trail of breadcrumbs so I can find my way back here."

Rationally I knew it was overkill to worry about being here in the airport with that psycho out there somewhere— and surely we'd left him, at least temporarily—in Paris. To worry about his being here was . . . well, he was succeeding in getting his message to me. He obviously wanted to keep us on edge, have us constantly worrying. That was part of his plan. Damn it, he was succeeding, too.

"Keep your eyes open," I said, knowing even as I spoke, it wasn't necessary. Elly was alert and aware. I had really become impressed with her on this trip and how well she handled the strain that underlay everything we did, saw, or sensed.

"Always," she said with a smile.

I tried to read more of Phil Bowie's book, but my mind kept going back to puzzling over who in the hell was this psycho, and what had triggered him. Something had to have set him off. He was obviously crazy—and I don't say this lightly—but he had to be crazy, doing what he was doing . . . teasing, tormenting, and—yes—killing. I couldn't help but think from that clipping he had left on Elly's windshield that he had killed the mother back near Raleigh, and in the presence of her son. Stabbed to death. The same type of killing inflicted on that innocent young woman on the Paris bridge. A long-bladed knife. Vicious.

After a while, Elly came back. Empty handed. "Would you like some ice cream? Or frozen yogurt?"

I smiled and shook my head.

She looked at me. "Thinking?"

"Yes . . . Can't help it."

"I know," she said. "I found myself watching everyone coming and going."

Muttering, almost to myself, I said, "I want to get rid of that son of a bitch. Put him behind us. Put him out of the way."

She nodded and sat down beside me. She didn't smile.

Time passed slowly but finally two agents came to the counter and started fooling with whatever it is they fool with, punching in something in a computer, talking on the phone or intercom, shuffling papers around. A number of passengers had appeared, filling up seats there at our gate. All headed to Norfolk and maybe beyond. At least four were obviously military. Norfolk's big Navy presence there made sense there would be service personnel traveling back and forth.

When the boarding procedure got underway, Elly and I both stood and flexed our shoulders, stretched our backs. Along with other passengers, we shuffled forward, boarding passes in hand.

Our seats were well forward on the relatively small plane, a CRJ. Nice aircraft and fairly new. Settled in and buckled up, Elly patted my wrist and said, "Leg number two."

We pushed back from the jetway, swung around and started taxiing for what seemed like miles. We got clearance on runway twenty-four and the pilot gave full power, accelerating quickly. We lifted off and began a turn around to the south and I leaned close to Elly and said, "Now it's leg number two."

After that trip across the Atlantic, the flight from Newark down to Norfolk, Virginia, seemed short. Knowing how much I enjoy looking out the window, Elly had again taken the aisle seat. I marveled at the coastline and how the water looked with the sun getting much lower over to the west but throwing light onto the sea.

A little over an hour of flight time, we crossed the Chesapeake Bay and I saw the bridge down below and how it stretched for miles, with a section disappearing under-water, and then reappearing to reach land on the other side. An engineering marvel. We landed at Norfolk International Airport—always at what seems like the absolute farthest end from baggage claim, and when we pulled up to the jetway and the captain had turned off the seatbelt sign so everyone was up and retrieving bags and other belongs, Elly leaned close to me and said, "And *now* we've completed leg number two."

Before walking to baggage claim, we paused long enough for Elly to call her mother. Then she spoke cheerily to Martin, who was already prepared to go to bed, and told him to sleep tight and that she would be home in the morning and she loved him and could hardly wait to see him. When she disconnected and handed me back my phone, she said, "I didn't tell him we're where we are. I think Mother is leaving it rather vague also, I hope."

After retrieved out luggage, we made our way to the garage to locate my car. This was a fairly easy task since I'd penciled in its location on the back of the parking ticket when we had arrived here last week. We loaded our suitcases and other stuff. I finally let go of my cloth briefcase with its valuables, including the ring, and put it in the rear also.

It was almost eight o'clock. I didn't want to think about what time it was back in Paris. Without making a show of it, Elly glanced at her watch, which I'm sure was still on Paris time. She made a face and shook her head.

Traffic was not bad on the loop around Norfolk and soon we were heading south on 168. At Hillcrest Parkway we exited to top off the tank at Wawa and avoid the Chesapeake Express toll road.

It would be at least nine-thirty when we got to my house at Kill Devil Hills.

We were both quiet as we continued driving. I could tell Elly mulled something over in her mind. She glanced out the passenger window from time to time. Finally she shifted toward me and spoke.

"I guess, Harrison, I've gotten rather used to the work that you do, the writing . . . about the subjects you write about." She gave the tiniest shake of her head. "Remember how just a year or so ago I kept urging you to be another kind of writer . . ." She chuckled, "Like even a romance writer? I know that from time to time, well actually frequently, it gets . . . gets real dicey. I guess that's the best way to put a nice picture to it. *Dicey*. Well, that's a prettier way of saying damn dangerous."

Keeping my eyes on the road, I managed quick glances at her. I was most intrigued with what she was saying and where it would lead.

"It's funny," she said, "At least it seems funny—not ha-ha funny—but strange maybe, that I don't fret over that anymore. Oh, I don't want danger, but I've fully accepted that this is what you do." She reached her left hand over and laid it gently on my forearm that rested on the steering wheel. "And I'm right here with you, and I'm going to be with you."

Then she turned toward me as much as the seatbelt would permit, and, with one eyebrow arched and a swash-buckling bravado in her voice, said, "And we're going to get that son of a bitch."

Chapter Twenty-Three

I couldn't help but smile. Here was the *new* Elly Pedersen, the tough Outer Banks gal. It was amazing how much more I'd come to admire her and know her on our few days in Paris. Yes, I was sure I loved her. Well, we were going to get to that when I presented her with that ring. She knew how I felt about her anyway, or at least, I thought she did, but I needed to say it, to tell her.

Traffic was not bad by the time we came to the intersection of US 158 and started what I felt was really and truly the final leg of our trip. We caught both traffic lights on green in Grandy and zipped past Venetia Huffman's Read 'em and Weep bookstore. The store was well stocked, and I was pleased to see an independent bookstore in Grandy. Wished her well, always.

A little later at Point Harbor, we approached the Wright Memorial Bridge over the Currituck Sound and Elly said, "Here we are! Home again, home again."

"Well, almost," I said. There was Southern Shores, Kitty Hawk, and then Kill Devil Hills, and I turned off the Bypass to the right and drove down to my little blue house. I pulled in under the carport, and with a sigh, I turned off the engine.

"I'll just take my carry-on," Elly said. "I've got something to sleep in and . . . extra things."

I got my suitcase out of the back and we trudged up the outside stairs to the kitchen door. A lamp, on a timer, illuminated the living room and the house looked homey to me. Glad to see it.

At the kitchen storm door I saw there was a note

jammed in at the edge of the door. I picked the note up and
unlocked the door and we went in. Flipping on the kitchen
light, I put my suitcase down and glanced at the note.

"A welcome home note?" Elly said. She moved around
me toward the living room.

"Not exactly," I said, and Elly stopped when she heard
the tone in my voice and looked back at me.

The note was on a piece of postcard stock paper, about
four or five inches square. It was a bit weathered as if it had
been there a few days. A message was in neat, hand-printed
block letters, done with a ballpoint pen.

The message said: *Reading this, you've discovered that
Paris was indeed "A Moveable Beast."*

A play on Hemingway's Paris sketches, *A Moveable
Feast.*

"What is it?" she said. She set her carry-on down and
came to my side. I handed her the note.

She studied it. Looked up at me. "Him?"

I nodded. "He put it there shortly after we'd left for
Paris . . . and obviously before he came over."

She gave the note back to me and I laid it carefully on
the dinette table I use as a desk. "No fingerprints on it—except mine and yours, I'm sure. I'll get Balls' people to check
it anyway."

"Hopefully he's still in Paris looking for us," Elly said.

"He'll be back. I'm sure of it."

"Not tonight, though. Let's go to bed."

I shrugged and managed a smile.

"I'm going to jump in the shower real quick." She
picked up her carry-on. "Sleeping in a T-shirt and panties if
that's okay."

"Sans T-shirt and panties would suit me."

"Get ready for bed," she said and headed to the bathroom. She stopped, dipped her head toward the kitchen
counter where Janey's cage usually rested. "Miss her," she
said.

"Me too. I'll get her from Misty's in the morning."

In bed, I thought about the note. Whoever he was, he knew of my fondness for Hemingway. After she lay there quietly for a while, Elly said, "He really is a beast."

"Yes, he is," I said.

Despite our exhaustion, it took a while before we drifted off to sleep.

We did sleep well and, though groggy in the morning, we were in fairly good shape. The fact that the sun was out, and the day sparkled, really helped.

I fixed coffee and opened the sliding glass door to the deck, breathed in the nice Outer Banks air.

Shortly after eight, Elly called her mother and promised her we'd be there soon and brunch would be wonderful. It was close to nine when we started to leave. Before we did, I called Misty and asked if it would be all right to pick up Janey later in the morning.

"Any time will be fine," she said. "I'll be here all day."

As we drove south on the Bypass, Elly said, "It seems like we've been gone longer than just a few days, doesn't it?"

I agreed. "Like coming back to a place that is only vaguely familiar."

"And I already miss Paris. Don't you?"

I smiled. "Yes, we could be getting that great onion soup at the Smoking Goose, watching the people go by, listening to the sounds of the city."

"But home is nice, too. And I do so want to see Martin . . . and Mother."

We swung around toward the causeway at Whalebone Junction, headed toward Pirates Cove and Manteo. Traffic was slow in Manteo but thinned out considerably on the west side of town approaching the airport and the left turnoff to Elly's house.

"Oh, it's good to be home," she said with joy in her voice when her house came into view. No sooner had I come to a complete stop, than Martin bounded out of the front door with a squeal of delight and raced to the car. Mrs. Pedersen stood in the doorway, a huge smile on her face.

There was a lot of hugging and grinning and welcome home sentiments and I got Elly's suitcase, and Elly, holding Martin's hand, who bounced up and down beside her, picked up her carry-on and told Martin she had something for him. We went inside and I gave Mrs. Pedersen a big hug. She smelled delightfully of country ham and biscuits.

Martin couldn't wait, so Elly sat on the sofa and opened her carry-on and took out a couple of the musical toys she had bought from Sarah. "I've got something else in my suitcase," she said to him, and to Mrs. Pedersen she said, "And you, too, Mother."

I carried Elly's suitcase to the bedroom. Mrs. Pedersen said she'd better finish up preparing breakfast and that it was almost ready.

The breakfast was sumptuous, as I knew it would be: homemade hot biscuits, real North Carolina country ham and not overcooked, butter and a jar of local honey, an assortment of cut up fresh fruit, large cheese and bacon-bits omelet, a scrambled egg for Martin. Orange juice, ice water, and a steaming pot of dark roast coffee.

I made a pig of myself. Elly didn't do too bad either. I finished off with a second coffee that washed down another biscuit topped with whipped butter and honey.

"Wonderful," I said to Mrs. Pedersen.

"Well, not like Paris, I don't suppose," she said.

"Our breakfasts there were nothing as good as this," I said.

"Not even close," Elly added.

Mrs. Pedersen began clearing the table. Elly rose to help her, but Mrs. Pedersen told her to sit back down. Elly said, "Okay," and then to her mother's back, Elly said, "Any excitement here while we've been gone?"

Mrs. Pedersen stopped, tried to think, "No, I guess not."

She chuckled a bit. "That is, if you discount Lauren's mother getting really upset, freaked out, because some man had parked for an hour or more out there on the road. She was convinced he was casing the place. This was, I think, the day after you all left." She shrugged one shoulder. "But you know how Lauren's mother is. Nervous Nellie."

Elly and I exchanged glances.

Elly's voice was as though she were trying to sound casual. "Did you see this person?"

From the kitchen, Mrs. Pedersen said, "No. He was just visible from Lauren's next door." Then, "It was nothing."

Martin played with one of his musical toys he had brought to the table. To Elly I mouthed a question: "She know anything about . . . ?"

Elly shook her head.

From the kitchen, Mrs. Pedersen called out, "Martin, show your mother and Mr. Harrison the picture you drew for them."

Martin, with a solemn expression on his face, got up from the table and went back to his room. He returned with two or three drawings. One was done on an off-white eight-by-eleven paper of heavy stock. He held it up for us to see.

I leaned forward and he handed the drawing to me. "Oh, this is very good, Martin. You're getting better all the time." And he was; he had graduated from stick-figure depictions of people to a somewhat stylized drawing of a man and a woman with the Eiffel Tower in the background. I showed the picture to Elly. "This is us! Your mother and me in Paris. Wonderful. Really good."

Elly bragged on him, too. He was, indeed, showing real promise and he definitely was improving.

The next one was of a man and woman and a small boy. "Wait," he said, and took the pencil he held in one hand and drew a halo over the little boy's head. He grinned at us.

Elly and I laughed.

"I want to keep this one, Martin," Elly said.

Silently, Martin nodded his approval.

Mrs. Pedersen called from the kitchen. "Did you show them the picture you did of school at recess?"

Martin went back to his room and came to us with a larger piece of paper, heavy stock. He offered the picture to me, probably because I was the closest. Elly looked on smiling.

He had drawn a whole scene, and I studied it carefully. A building, which I assumed was the school, was in the background. In the foreground a monkey-bar gym set had four young children climbing on it. The children were rendered very well, somewhat stylistic or impressionistic, but certainly several steps up from stick figures. To the left in the picture there was a large tree that was done very well. Most children his age drew trees that looked like vertical lollipops. This one had limbs and leaves, the works.

"This is excellent, Martin. I mean that."

Then I noticed the man. Standing near the trunk of the tree was a man—a man wearing a rather long coat.

Before passing the picture over to Elly, I said, "Who is this, Martin?" and pointed to the figure of the man.

Martin shrugged. "A man. He was just standing there when I drew it. At recess."

Elly took the picture. I watched her face. She bit down on her lower lip. Then she looked up at me, pain in her face. Back to Martin, she said with an unsteady voice, "When did you draw this, Martin?"

Martin cocked his head to one side looking at his picture Elly held. "When you all went to Paris."

Her voice still strained, Elly said, "These are all very nice, Martin. Really good." She was having difficulty.

When Martin took his artwork back to his room, Elly whispered to me, "That scares me, Harrison."

I nodded.

"I don't want to leave him alone. Not any more. Not for any time."

"He's safe here with your mother, I'm sure." Actually, I wasn't at all sure.

When Martin came back, I said, "Did the man talk to anyone? The man in the picture, by the tree."

He shook his head. "He wasn't there long. Maybe he was somebody's daddy."

"Probably," I said.

Elly was still worried when I got ready to leave. I could see it in her face.

I thanked Mrs. Pedersen again for the breakfast.

"We've got to have this thing end," Elly whispered, her voice urgent and steely. Then she said in a more normal tone, "You'll be calling Agent Twiddy?"

"Yes. Bring him up to date. On everything," I added. We walked to the front door. "Have to get Janey and unpack, too."

Elly put her hand on the front doorknob. "Do you think Agent Twiddy will come down?"

"I have a feeling he will," I said. Balls did investigations throughout northeast North Carolina, and beyond. I'm not sure exactly how many years Balls had been with the State Bureau of Investigations, but probably close to two decades. He was five or so years older than me. He was fond of saying that he got his law experience started as a foot patrolman in Northern Virginia and spent a number of years "rattling doors," a reference to walking the streets at night in a city and making sure storefront doors were locked securely.

When I got home, I went immediately upstairs, picked up my suitcase from the bedroom floor and flopped it up on the bed. From the suitcase I rummaged around for the box of Belgian chocolates to deliver next door to Misty and retrieve Janey.

After visiting just a few minutes with Misty, I returned with Janey and set her cage in its customary place on the kitchen counter. She bobbed her head happily and chirped full volume. "You have fun over there, Janey?" I said.

"Shit, shit," she said.

"You like Misty? She good to you?"

"Bitch," Janey said, once again completing her entire vocabulary.

Then I called Balls. After three rings when I thought it was going to voice mail, he picked up and grumbled, "Yeah?"

Ah, good to hear the ol' Balls again.

I brought him up to date, including the handwritten note we had found last night. Telling it all it took a while and he was quiet almost the entire time.

Stopping to take a breath, I said, "So what do you think?"

"He's not through with you."

"I figured that."

"He's gonna be pissed off that you slipped out of Paris ahead of schedule. That might up his timetable."

"You think he's really got a timetable?"

"Yeah. He's too methodical not to have."

I was quiet a moment. So was Balls. Then I said, "When are you coming this way?"

"Monday morning, early. I've got a case down there anyway . . . and I'd like to hang around there much as I can." He chuckled. "Try to keep your ass outta trouble."

"Breakfast Monday morning? Henry's?"

"Yeah, the three-egg omelet. Loaded. You're buying."

After we hung up, I sat there a minute or two. It would be good to see Balls. I always felt good when he was around.

Then I sighed and stood. Time to go downstairs and rummage through my old files from the writing courses, see if I could come up with a roster of students.

Maybe, just maybe this psycho was one of them . . . and a name would spark something. Give me a clue.

Chapter Twenty-Four

When I unlocked the utility room door, my first thought was that I really needed to get in here soon and straighten the place up. The utility room, which houses the washer and dryer and hot water tank, is under the house at the end of the carport. Such utility rooms are usual features on these small beach box houses of a couple or three bedrooms.

And my utility room, like that of many others I'm sure, serves as a depository for a bunch stuff I don't know what to do with at the moment. That included two sagging boxes of notes and files I couldn't quite bring myself around to discarding. Right now I was glad I hadn't trashed these files, which among other things, did indeed contain notes on writing classes I had taught—and maybe a roster or two of former students.

I was lucky. Near the top of a large cardboard box two smaller boxes contained file notes from classes I had taught. Leafing through one, I found at least two sheets that had served as rosters of attendees. Grinning, I backed out of the utility room, locked the door, and carried my files upstairs.

Sitting at my dinette table/desk, I spread the notes in front of me. One of the classes was on nonfiction and the other hints on writing fiction, along with pitfalls to avoid. Actually, reading through my notes I was rather impressed, yes, a bit proud. A stated goal of the nonfiction class was to have the students try to place a feature story or news item in a local media. Quite a bit of success in that, too. There was the student I'd almost remembered, the one who had landed a job with a local newspaper. I recognized her name now:

JoAnne Blanchard.

Another student, Mary Ann Little, was already working part-time at a weekly in Camford Courthouse when she enrolled in the class and basically wanted to sharpen her writing skills. Our paths had crossed a few times since that class. The other names of those taking nonfiction did not spark any particular memory. Certainly, none sent a shiver of foreboding that a psycho lurked here.

I studied the file on the fiction class, where the emphasis was on several basics in short stories or novels. Character development was a must, of course, and that plot would follow character. Emphasis should not be first and foremost on plot, I told them, because the characters, if developed, want something and obstacles stand in their way, plot comes about as they try—successfully or unsuccessfully—to attain the desired goal.

Setting was another topic, and I remembered spending a lot of time on dialogue and having fun with that—how dialogue should do one of two things: delineate character or advance the story, and never use dialogue as an information dump.

Time was spent too on editing and avoiding adverbs and watching for overuse of certain words.

In going over my notes, I realized I had gotten caught up in what I had been teaching and enjoying reminiscing. But then I jerked myself around to get back to studying the list of attendees, which was what I was supposed to be doing, not lingering over how clever I was in the class and how much I enjoyed the whole process of trying to learn to write.

Studying the names, however, didn't do much of anything. My roster was not well done, and I wasn't even sure it was complete. Scribbled names that, try as I might, conjured up very little. I found a second sheet that contained names of attendees. Was this another class? It could have well been. Hell, then there was a third sheet with a few more names. Not very well organized. I did recognize one or two of these names.

There was a young man named Jonathan Clayton who had a great deal of talent. A couple of years later he got his first novel published. And then there was a studious young man named Lawrence Swafford, who worked diligently and maybe had some talent; he was surely dedicated to finding out. There were two women I vaguely remembered as being dreamy and poetic and smoking a lot of cigarettes.

But among the group, a psycho? I drew a blank. Concentrating, I tried to remember the classrooms, where students sat; faces were dim or not there at all. I could remember that two of the woman sat close to the front and one man always lurked somewhat sullenly at the back of the room. Except for those few names that I did recall, nothing else came to mind. Well, so much for this exercise.

The psycho was still out there somewhere—maybe on his way back from Paris and I was no closer to discovering who it might be than I was in the beginning.

I started to carry the files back to the utility room but decided to do that the next time I went downstairs. Besides, I might make a new file with highlights of topics like dialogue or setting or character development to use in teaching another class in the near future.

Janey had been quiet the entire time I was going over the files—or maybe I had concentrated so much on what I was doing I had not heard her. Learning to write and concentrate in a busy newsroom will do that for you. You can tune out everything except what is before you. When I stood, she definitely began to chirp. I spoke to her and she did her head-bobbing dance.

Then it occurred to me that Jonathan Clayton, that budding writer who got his first novel published a year or so after the class, might have more recollections of people in the class than I did. After his novel was published—a coming-of-age story set in Raleigh called *A Dance in Time*—he and I had exchanged correspondence, and at least one or two phone conversations. I still had his email address. I'd drop him a note telling him I was trying to recall something about the other students and wondered if he could help me out. That'd be enough detail to tell him. So before I did anything else, I sent him an email, asking him if we could talk.

My body was still a bit confused over what time of day or night it was. But I was determined to go about my business as if there was no such thing as jetlag. One of the first orders of business, after setting aside those files, was to get in there and unpack, put clothes away and do a small load of laundry.

But by two o'clock I began to feel a bit worn out and knew it was time to eat a bite. As good and filling as it was, the brunch at Elly's wouldn't last forever. Then, too, I needed to get back on a schedule of meals and other routines.

That evening I talked again with Elly on the phone. She was quite involved with Martin and puttering around the house. We agreed we'd get together tomorrow night. She needed to spend time at home and enjoy being with Martin.

When we ended the conversation, I thought about tomorrow evening. Maybe we could take one of our walks out on the beach. It had been awhile. A golden evening along hard-packed sand at the edge of the ocean. Just the two of us. Maybe the perfect time to present her with the ring. I felt good about that.

Late Sunday morning I had been clearing up emails and handling necessary correspondence when the phone rang. I went across the living room. For once I didn't have to step over the neck of my bass fiddle because it remained upright secured in its stand.

Checking the ID, I saw it was a Raleigh area code from J. Clayton. With a smile I answered, and right away, in an almost booming cheery voice, Jonathan Clayton said, "Why aren't you in church?" He certainly sounded more mature and confident in himself than he did when he was in my writing class. Well, being the author of a well-received first novel will do it for most people.

Going right along with him, I answered, "I got special dispensation from the preacher this morning when I told him I was awaiting a call from the renowned author, Jonathan Clayton."

A bit more banter back and forth between us. Then I asked him what he was working on and he immediately got serious. "Actually a prequel to the Raleigh novel. Same family, a few years earlier, and set in Asheville." He paused a moment. "Tough to write but I think it will be good. Hope so."

"I know it will be," I said.

"And you?" he asked.

"Still doing a lot of crime writing, but have had moderate success with that. Do have a novel I'm finishing up, and some short stories."

"Moderate success is probably the understatement of today," he said. "I know about the books and the TV movie on one of them. Maybe two."

"Been lucky," I said.

"Yeah . . . and talent and hard work have had nothing to do with it. Right?" Then he said, "And now that we're through telling each other how great we are, we'll get down to why you contacted me. You said in your email you were trying to get a rundown on some of the students who were in our class—for what? Six weeks?"

I was still amazed at how he had come into his own; he didn't seem at all like the shy, introverted young man who sat there in the classroom taking notes, his eyes on me the whole time, drinking in and absorbing everything I said.

"Yes," I said. "Of course I remember your name and that of Lawrence Swafford, but that's about all. The rest of them seem pretty vague."

"You do have a roster of the names?"

"Well, sort of . . ."

He was quiet a moment or two. "Why, Mr. Weaver?"

"What do you mean?"

He gave a short chuckle. "Like you used to say about Hemingway's iceberg theory of writing, I don't believe you're telling me all of the story. Your iceberg is down more than the customary ninety percent."

"Jonathan, make it 'Weav,' and drop the Mister."

"Okay. Old habits, you know."

"Yes, I owe you more of an explanation." I took a breath. "Tell the truth, someone has been . . . well, stalking me. And there's some indication it might possibly have been someone in one of the writing classes I've taught, and certainly someone who knew me several years ago . . . when I still smoked cigarettes, Kool cigarettes."

"Stalking you?" Again, a short chuckle. "I'll bet it's one or both of two young gals who sat in the front of the class." He was having fun. "They couldn't keep their eyes off you. They had real crushes on you." His grin was virtually visible over the phone. "Do people still say 'crushes'?"

Now it was my time to give a little chuckle. "Yes, I remember them. I had a difficult time keeping my eyes off of them, especially the way they sat, and crossed and uncrossed their legs."

"Yeah, I'm sure that made it hard for you."

"Okay, enough of the double-entendre."

"All right, we'll get serious." His voice took on a more subdued tone. "Apparently this is something that worries you or at least concerns you enough to get in touch with me."

"Yes, you're correct. Without going into any details at this point, I wondered if you recall anyone in the class who might . . . well, who might have taken an intense dislike to me."

"Wow. This does sound serious." I could tell he thought for a moment or two. "Tell you the truth, Mr. Wea . . . Weav . . . most of the faces in the class are vague to me, too. I remember Lawrence Swafford and the two women and some guy who always sat at the back of the room, looking like the tortured poet—or just sullen, not sure which. I don't remember his name except that it sounded so fancy, his name did, that I figured he'd made it up."

I said, "What about Swafford? I know he was trying really diligently, but rather plodding. And I'm saying 'plodding,' not 'plotting' as in a story."

"Oh, you don't know? He was the only one of us who didn't need a day job. Had plenty of money, apparently from his family, and after the course he told me over a beer one night that he had applied for and been accepted to the Sorbonne in Paris and he was moving there to pursue what he said was his 'writing passion and career.' And he did just that."

I gripped the phone a bit tighter. Money, didn't have to work, free to travel, familiar with Paris. I was intrigued.

Jonathan Clayton continued. "He writes under the name of Larry Strong. Maybe you've seen something by him. He published two novels—at least they're called novels. When you say *plodding* rather than *plotting*, you don't know how close you were to the truth. I'm not sure who published them. He sent me one and I read it, or tried to read it."

Jonathan gave another one of those mirthless chuckles. "He should have paid more attention to your segment on self-editing."

"Where is he now?" I tried to make my voice sound only casually interested.

"Oh, he's still in Paris, or at least most of the time. Apparently he's convinced some people over there that he's a well-respected and mildly famous American writer."

I said, "I'll look him up."

"I can send you his email address if you want it."

"Please."

"Other than that, Weav, I can't remember much about the other students. But I do remember that class, and I want you to know how much it has meant to me and continues to mean to me. I go over time and again things you said about, oh, everything from dialogue to mood setting to self-editing."

We talked a bit longer and he told me more about his work-in-progress. Before we signed off he said he hoped I would write another what he called "literary" novel like my first two books. I told him I was doing that with short stories. It was good talking with him, and my initial reaction to learning about Lawrence Swafford, now known as Larry Strong, as a possibility as a psycho had faded a bit. And Jonathan Clayton had promised to send me his email address. Whether I would really need it was debatable, what with searches on the Internet that I could easily do.

Later during the day, I did just that and found a website for "Larry Strong Author." A fancy website it was, too, with a lot of what we call BSP, or Blatant Self-Promotion. Contained on the website was a list of Upcoming Events, which included speaking engagements this week in Paris and then later in the month an appearance at a convention in New York. Yes, he did get around and was certainly doing a good job of making himself sound like a prominent and successful author. Or at least his hired publicist was doing a good job, and I'm sure with Lawrence's guidance.

I shook my head because, like Jonathan Clayton had indicated, Lawrence—or Larry Strong—was not one we would think of as talented, or even skillful.

Perusing his website a bit more, the feeling grew that, while he might be many things, a psycho stalking me was not one of them.

But the stalker was still out there. Somewhere. I would eventually uncover him. I was sure of that.

Perhaps I was right. Or perhaps he would reveal himself. Sooner rather than later.

Chapter Twenty-Five

With my body still wrestling with adjusting to Outer Banks time and not the six hours earlier in Paris, I was up before six Monday morning, wide awake. Another beautiful sunny day with hardly any wind at all. I stood out on the deck and breathed in the ocean air, always imaging I could smell and taste the salt off the sea.

Ah, the ocean. My place of reverence, my spiritual home church.

I debated calling Elly before she left for work. Decided not to because maybe Martin or Mrs. Pedersen were sleeping, and I'd checked with her last night before going to bed, just to hear her voice and tell her goodnight.

I finished my coffee, went back inside for a shower and to get dressed to meet Balls at seven-thirty at Henry's.

I drove north on the Bypass for less than a mile to the popular breakfast restaurant. The parking lot was crowded but plenty of spaces remained. Knowing Balls and his care for that vintage Thunderbird of his, he would park back on the "south forty" away from other cars, and he'd reverse into his space so he could, as always, make a fast gunning getaway if he needed to.

Standing on the front porch of the restaurant, I watched the traffic and waited only a few minutes before Balls' Thunderbird rumbled onto the lot, his engine making a subdued but powerful throaty sound.

I couldn't help but grin a happy greeting as I watched that big bear of a man come toward me. He was powerful, yet moved with a certain athletic grace that you wouldn't expect.

He extended a paw-like hand and gave me a scowling once over appraisal. "You don't look too bad for having been in Paris with your sweetie for a week. Well, bags under your eyes. Probably walk with a limp. Enough more wrinkles on your face to look like a waded up newspaper."

"Yes, good to see you, too, Balls."

We went inside and spoke to pretty co-owner Linda. She was behind the counter at the register. "Your hair is lovely as always," I said, and she said, "Thank you, kind sir," and probably unconsciously brushed the palm of her right hand across the side of her hair, which is a lively gray and has been prematurely gray for years. Linda had one of the hostesses guide us to a booth on the right side, next to a window.

Balls sat so he could keep an eye toward the front. "Just can't help but flirt with the ladies, can you?" he said.

"I like her," I said.

"You like all women."

"True. But it's all innocent adoration."

"Yeah, right."

The waitress came up quickly. We exchanged good mornings. I couldn't remember her name, but I'd seen her here several times before. She was comfortably husky, with short red hair and a big smile. Freckles ran across the bridge of her nose.

We had menus, but didn't really need them. Balls ordered his usual: the three-egg omelet, stuffed with ham, cheese, crab and anything else they might have in the kitchen, hash brown potatoes, a double-order of white bread toast, butter and jelly, a tall glass of tomato juice with crushed ice, and coffee. The waitress pointed out that jelly and butter were in packets on the table.

I got a ham and cheese omelet, biscuits, and just ice water, no lemon.

When the waitress hurried away with our order, Balls said, "All right, fill me in."

I did just that, most of which I had relayed to him in different segments over a period of days. New, was my checking with the roster of my writing classes and the conversation with Jonathan Clayton.

By the time I'd finished, with hardly any interruptions from Balls, the waitress appeared with our food. Balls started in immediately.

Speaking with a hefty morsel of food in his mouth, he said, "Mr. Psycho's gonna be pissed that you slipped out of Paris ahead of schedule." He washed the food down with a slug of tomato juice. "He probably had something else planned for you there."

"That's what we were afraid of."

He looked up at me. "You were wise to leave early." He nodded. "Glad you took my advice."

I was not making as much progress with my food as Balls was, and I stopped eating again. "So what do you think will happen next?"

Balls toyed with two or three of the jelly packets, set one on top of the other, his eyes on the packets as if it took great concentration; but he was probably not even aware of what he was doing. He was thinking. That's what he was doing.

He pushed the jelly aside with the fingers of his left hand and looked across at me, his face set, cop-like. "I think he's tired of fooling with you. Tired of this foreplay of his. He's pissed off and angry because you slipped out of his grasp, and he needs to feel superior. He needs to be the one in charge, the one calling the shots, keeping you on edge . . . and Elly, too. Don't forget her."

"I can't forget her, and I worry about her and my putting her in danger. And tell you the truth, Balls, no matter what I'm doing, that stalker is always in my mind. Maybe in the back of my mind sometimes . . . but there. Always." I sighed and shook my head. "I'm damn tired of it, Balls. Really. Damn tired of it."

"I gotta feeling you may not have to wait much longer."

He crammed a half a piece of toast, loaded with jelly, into his mouth and chewed away. "But you know we gotta be careful what we wish for."

"I know," I said, and picked at my omelet.

We were quiet for a minute or two. Balls had almost finished his breakfast. The waitress came over and refilled his coffee. She wanted to know if we needed anything else. I thanked her and said no. She put the check on the table, more or less between us, and Balls glanced at it and then pushed it toward me with the fingers of his left hand.

"You're paying," he said.

I expected to. "Coffee good?" I asked, tipping my head toward his cup.

"Yeah. Strong. Used not to be. Is now."

I signaled our Ms. Redhead and motioned for coffee by pointing to Balls' cup and then myself. She smiled and nodded. My coffee mug appeared promptly. "Okay, Balls, what are you working on here at the Outer Banks."

He took a loud slurp of his coffee. "None of your damn business."

I gave a half-grin to myself. "Aw, come on, Balls."

"Okay. You ain't gonna write about anything until I give the word."

"As per usual," I said. This was a long-standing agreement between the two of us and it had never been violated. Wasn't going to be.

"Odell has opened a cold case file. Wants to take another shot at it 'cause something else has come up."

"Oh, boy . . . You're really telling me a whole lot."

"Don't be a smart ass." He gave a touch of a shrug. "Don't guess Odell'd mind if I told you more, though. Odell sorta likes you."

Chief Deputy Odell Wright was one of the first black members of the Dare County Sheriff's Department. He had risen through the ranks with hard work and dedication—and a lot of skill as an investigator.

Balls continued. "You probably remember. Young woman was found in the burned beach house. Looked like she died in the fire but turns out she was murdered before the fire was started. No arrests. Couple of suspects who had rock-solid alibis. Now been another one, same M.O. in Currituck County."

"Yes," I said, "I've heard about both of them."

He pushed his empty coffee cup away. "You 'bout through?"

I took a final sip. "Yes."

But he didn't get up immediately. Instead, he looked steadily at me and said, "Keep your eyes open. And I wouldn't let your sweetie be anywhere she might be exposed, in danger." He shook his head. "This bastard's gonna be making his move soon. I got a feeling."

"Yes, I'm worried about that too."

"If he's like I think he is, he's gotta prove that just because you escaped him in Paris, doesn't mean you can get away from him here at the Outer Banks." He sat up straighter, ready to stand. "And I think he's the one who killed that young mother near Raleigh—the one he left the news clipping about—and we're pretty solid he killed that girl on the bridge in Paris."

"And threw down a beret just like the one Elly had bought," I said. "To let me know."

We both stood and I picked up the check.

"I'll be here in Dare County most of the week," he said. "Keep that phone with you and have me on speed dial."

I don't think I'd ever seen Balls as concerned. Yes, even worried.

With an inward shudder, I realized I trusted his sense of what might be on the not-too-distant horizon.

Chapter Twenty-Six

Outside, we came to Balls' car. He leaned against the front fender, and I stood with my back to the southeast to keep the sun out of my eyes.

I told him I planned to go down to Manteo also.

"Don't be bugging me there at the courthouse," he said. "Just spend time with your sweetie."

"Yes, I'm going to see her." I looked over at Balls. "I'm going to caution her not to go anywhere without telling me and best not to go anywhere except to and from work. Lock her car during the day—I doubt if she ever does—and keep Martin close to home also, and under close supervision."

Then I paused. Balls kept silent. I shook my head back and forth several times. "Shit, Balls, but I'm tired of this." I had my fists balled. "I want to get that son of a bitch."

We were quiet a beat or two. Then he said, "I can see somebody getting pissed off enough at me to cause me harm."

He gave something of a half-hearted grin. "But you just ain't the kind what causes that much hate." He stroked his mustache briefly. "Remember what I told you about psychos: it could be triggered by what the guy thinks is some sort a slight . . . or even success that he thinks should be his."

I didn't say anything.

"That's probably it. Somebody jealous. Maybe one of your fellow egghead writers?"

I sighed. "I've tried my best to come up with any suspect—anyone at all—and I don't do anything but draw a blank."

I stepped back from his car as Balls got in, started the engine. He nodded a goodbye and I raised a hand as he drove away.

When I got home I checked on Janey; spoke to her, which prompted her to chirp and dance around in her cage. "Okay, Janey, I'll be back after a while, but I'm going to Manteo and see Elly."

"Bitch," Janey chirped.

"That's no way to talk. She's very nice to you.

"Shit," Janey said.

I grinned—maybe for the first time fully that day—and got ready to leave.

In Manteo I found a parking space across the street from Jamie's Downtown Books. So I went in there before going to the courthouse. Wanted to speak to Jamie and tell her about Brian Spence's Abbey Bookshop in Paris.

Jamie was behind the counter doing something on her computer when I came in. "Ah, *bonjour*," she said.

"And *bonjour* to you," I replied.

She came around the counter and gave me a hug. "Welcome back."

Then I told her about Brian Spence's decision to scrap the idea of teaching and instead opened a bookstore in Paris. Jamie's eyes lit up at the story. "Good for him," she said.

I asked her what she was reading and what she recommended. Quite a list, and I came away with two more books before I left to go to see Elly at the courthouse. First, though, I put the two books in my car on the backseat. And I made sure I locked the car. Got to get in the habit of that.

Before going in the front of the courthouse and turning into Elly's office at the Register of Deeds, I had glanced to my right at Balls' Thunderbird parked in one of the reserved spots on Budleigh Street. He had to be upstairs with Deputy Wright, maybe Sheriff Albright. Yes, I would leave them alone, not bug them, as Balls had cautioned.

Elly greet me with a big smile. She and coworker Becky

were alone in the office. Upon seeing me, Becky reached under the counter that separated us and produced the beret Elly and I had bought in Paris. She plopped it on her head and said, "How do I look?"

"Real Parisian," I said. Her grin stretched across her round face and tufts of her blonde hair stuck out from the sides of the beret, set at a jaunty angle.

"I love it," she beamed.

I couldn't help but think about the identical beret that had been tossed beside the murdered woman on Pont L'Archeveche, Paris. Just the same, I pushed that thought out of my mind the best I could and concentrated on happy Becky. Elly watched my face and I'm sure she knew the inner struggle I was going through.

A paralegal from one of the law offices came in and Becky whipped off her beret and went to help the woman. Elly and I moved to the far end of the counter. Talking softly I asked her when we could get together. "Like a real date," I said.

With a knowing smile, she said, "I know what you have in mind."

"Oh, yes," I said. "You know, dinner, maybe a movie . . ."

"Um-huh." Then she got more serious. "How about Wednesday night?"

"Fine."

"I want to spend as much time as I can with Martin. Make him feel reassured I'm not taking off again."

"I understand," I said. Then I told her how I wanted her to stay in touch with me and not go anywhere that wasn't really necessary, keep her car locked, and the doors at home.

"You make it sound scary," she whispered.

"I think it is . . . and so does Balls . . . until this character is locked up or something."

I could see the depression creeping over face. "I'm tired of it, aren't you?"

"Yes, I certainly am. And I am so very sorry that I have

probably got you involved when you didn't need to be."

She glanced to make sure the paralegal and Becky were still engaged and she touched my forearm lightly. "Well, I'm *involved* with you . . . and whatever you are involved in."

We agreed on Wednesday night and that I would pick her up just before six and we'd go to dinner. "Yes, maybe even a movie . . . if you want to tell your mother that."

She got a half-smile on her face. "Always planning, aren't you, Harrison?"

"See you then," I said. "But we'll be talking on the phone before then, of course."

"Be careful," she said.

"Remember what I said about locking up and everything."

She nodded and I left.

When I stepped out on the front porch of the courthouse, I caught myself looking both ways, up and down the street, making sure no psychos lurked about. Both of us were sick of this. I wanted to get it over.

Back at my house I had a message from Rose, my editor. She was always hungry for more copy. But she had my latest and there were no other deadlines at the moment pushing me. I called her.

Rose answered, with a slight cough from the cigarette I knew she was smoking. That Brooklyn accent of hers coming through, she said, "Wanted to tell you, Weaver, that this piece is great. So good, matter of fact, I want you to expand on the section about the woman's motivation . . . the stuff that starts on page thirty-nine."

I chuckled at her. "There may be a 'this is great' and at the same time there's always a 'however.' You never disappoint, Rose."

She cackled a laugh and a cough simultaneously.

"Happy to oblige, Rose."

"That's what I like about working with a Southerner," she said. "You're always so damn polite and ready to oblige."

I enjoyed her. "Speaking of different regions of the country, one thing I've noticed over the years, Rose, is that Northerners are never as angry as they sound and Southerners are never really as friendly as they sound."

She got a kick out of that. "Brilliant, Weaver . . . now get that rewriting done before I kick you in the butt . . ."

I almost always felt good after talking with Rose. I had worked with her for close to ten years now, and she had seen me through some tough periods as well as some quite nice successes.

The section for further writing that she mentioned was one I'd sensed at the time needed to be expanded. Always follow your instincts. I tried to stick with that, but not always successfully. I'd get to it by tomorrow at the latest. In fact, I started a stab at it later that same afternoon.

Of course I talked over the phone with Elly that evening and then she called me later to wish me goodnight before she went to bed. She had read Martin two stories. She said she worried about the picture he had drawn of the man at the school yard. I told her I was speaking with Sheriff Albright and Deputy Odell Wright about increasing police presence around the school, and at her house.

"So don't be surprised when you and your mother see a deputy's cruiser drifting by."

"Thank you, Harrison," she said.

When I got in bed, I started reading one of the two books I'd bought that day from Jamie. This was *The Great Alone* by Kristin Hannah. Such good writing. I marveled at how all of us use essentially the same words that we arrange in sentences and then paragraphs—then how come some of the words strung together are so much better than others? What is it about the writing of some people, like Kristin Hannah, that makes what you are reading so much more moving, so much more awe-inspiring than similar words put together differently? Ah, Harrison, this is a question for the critics and the English professors, not just an ink-stained wretch like yourself.

I closed the book and went to sleep—but not before vowing that I would do better at using words in such a fashion that someone, somewhere, sometime, would give a sigh of admiration at the way I'd put those familiar words together, and made them sing.

The next day, Tuesday, I finished rewriting the section Rose wanted expanded, and shipped it electronically off to her in New York.

Shortly before eleven that morning I was surprised to have a call from Elly. She rarely called from work.

Her voice was very soft and a bit muffled as if she cupped a palm partially over the phone's mouthpiece. She was in her office, she said, but standing at the far end of the counter.

"It's probably nothing," she said, "and I guess I'm as edgy as you can get, but there was a man standing across the street for some minutes a while ago and he kept staring at the courthouse—and it seemed he was staring at this corner office."

I leaned forward in the little rattan chair by the telephone. "What did he look like?"

"That's just it. There was nothing unusual about him. He just reminded me of the way you described that person you saw in Paris and the one you saw at your musical job at Scarborough Faire. He was tall and he wore a thigh-length windbreaker or coat of some kind."

"Is he still there?" I heard her move about. I assumed she moved closer to the window in her office, the one that looks out the front of the courthouse.

"No, he's gone." She gave a short, self-deprecating laugh. "I guess my imagination is working overtime." Sounding like she was doing a good job of convincing herself, she said, "So somebody is looking at the courthouse. Well, it's a historic building, right? Why shouldn't somebody look at it?"

"When you get off work this evening, maybe you can get Becky to walk to your car with you." Then I said, "You staying in for lunch?"

"Yes, I brought something from home. And I parked close this morning . . . and yes, I locked the car."

There was no question about it. Both of us were on edge. That son of a bitch had accomplished that, certainly. He had us worrying all the time.

And I worried again that night. Again probably needlessly. It was after Elly and I had had our goodnight telephone conversation, I stepped out on the deck and looked up at the stars. A beautiful, clear night.

There at the end of the cul-de-sac I saw the taillights of a parked vehicle. The taillights were not high enough to be a pickup truck. More like a sedan or small SUV. The vehicle didn't move. I watched a moment. I was backlit from my lamp and other lights in my house. Then the vehicle moved away. Probably nothing.

After I got ready for bed, I returned to the dark living room and went out on the deck again. The vehicle was back, at least the taillights looked the same. I came inside, bolted shut the sliding glass door, and watched. About three minutes later, the vehicle moved slowly away.

I went to bed. Before I cut out my bedroom lamp, I took my revolver out of the bedside table drawer, removed it from its somewhat oily sock, and laid it atop the table. It was loaded with .32 caliber rounds.

Chapter Twenty-Seven

Wednesday morning early, I went outside and walked up to the end of the cul-de-sac where the vehicle had been parked last night. I wasn't sure what I could find but I thought there might be something, and I was right.

There, barely smoked, were three Kool cigarette butts.

Yes, it had been him out there. Stalking. Keeping an eye on me. Prodding, teasing, getting bolder.

I walked slowly back to my house. There are only three houses on my cul-de-sac, and a vacant lot on one side and a rarely used house on the other. The house behind me, which faces the other street, has also been vacant now for several months.

Inside, I contemplated practicing the bass but gave up on that idea. I just wasn't in the mood. I looked at it there, standing upright in its stand close to the end of the sofa. Its wood gleamed from the sunlight coming through the sliding glass doors.

I checked the weather. It had been so pretty the past few days but this evening a front was expected to creep in and bring a bit of rain. Maybe it would hold off long enough for Elly and me to walk out on the beach after dinner and I could present her with that ring. Seemed like something got in the way of that every time.

During the day I called her and suggested dinner at the Black Pelican. There was a beach access across the Beach Road from the restaurant. Be perfect—if the rain held off.

I didn't tell her about the car parked last night. But I did call Balls and gave him an update.

He said, "I agree with you. He's getting bolder, more sure of himself . . . or either he's reached the point he just doesn't give a damn." He paused. "And that's not good."

I told him Elly and I were going out tonight for dinner.

"Rather you just stayed at her house," he said.

"I'll be alert," I said. "You better believe it."

By five-thirty that afternoon I was ready to head over to Elly's when the phone rang. I checked caller ID and didn't recognize the number, probably a robo-call or cell phone. I started not to answer, but I did. No one responded. I sensed someone was on the line. I waited. I didn't say anything else. As I was about to ease the handset back in its cradle, a whispery male voice, slight cultured Southern accent, breathed the words, "I've decided how it ends."

Anger flashed over me and I started to lash out verbally with a string of cuss words, but the phone went dead.

I delayed driving over to Elly's long enough to call Balls and tell him about the phone call.

"Crap," he said. "Bastard's getting real pushy." Then, "You still going out to eat?"

"Yes, I'm not going to let that son of a bitch run my life."

Balls was silent. Then he said, "No one operates as well when they're angry. Cool down. And keep your cool. Remember, you gotta stay focused . . . and cool."

I took a deep breath. "I'll do my best."

Driving over to Elly's I debated whether to say anything about these latest so-called encounters—the parked vehicle, cigarette butts, and now the phone call.

I realized I owed her that, the keeping her in the loop. Even though it might ruin the evening—and I did have the ring in my pocket.

When I got to her house and we said our goodbyes to Martin and Mrs. Pedersen and got in the car, the first thing Elly asked was, "What's the matter, Harrison?"

Although I always loved the way she said my name, I

wasn't concentrating on that. I thought about the warnings from Balls and the other things that had happened. So I told her what was the matter as we drove through Manteo and headed up to the Black Pelican. I brought her completely up to date, and I told her Balls was worried too but I was determined to continue living our lives.

She was silent for only a moment before she thrust her chin forward, her face defiant. "No, we can't let him control and dictate our lives."

Whether she actually felt truly that brave, I don't know. I admired her for it, but I was not sure I felt that brave either. He was winning, certainly for now.

We were both determined during the meal to keep our spirits up and we talked about how nice it was to eat at places like the Smoking Goose in Paris.

"I'm ready to go back," she said. Hidden in that statement, I figured, was a desire to get away from that which hung over us here, ignoring the fact that the pall of gloom had shrouded us there as well.

When we finished eating and I'd signaled for the check, I looked out the window beside our table to see whether the forecast for rain had materialized. I couldn't really tell. Dusk was coming on fast. It did look like a mist was developing.

I said, "I was hoping we could take a walk on the beach . . ." I leaned closer to the window. ". . . but I'm not sure if the weather is holding."

Elly peered at the window. "I believe it may have started. Or is getting ready to."

I touched the outside of my right side pocket. Felt the bulge of the ring, which now rested in a small black velvet pouch. The tiny box I had transported it around in had started feeling too bulky for the lightweight clothes we were now wearing at the Outer Banks.

"Elly, let's just go over to my house for a while. Do you mind?"

She reached across the table and touched my wrist. Her

slim, delicate fingers felt cool. Her hands were like those of a violinist. She brightened the table with a smile. "I thought you'd never ask, Harrison." Then she added, more seriously, "We can't stay long. I really need to be home. You understand."

It was now fully dark and misting rain as we left the Black Pelican and drove up the long block on Kitty Hawk Road to the Bypass, waited for the light, and turned left. We caught another light at Helga Street. I liked to say *Helga* with a fake German accent. It reminded me of "Cabaret" and Joel Grey. No one would ever play the androgynous master of ceremonies better than he did.

Elly patted my thigh. "And the writer gives a mysterious smile over hidden thoughts . . . that are probably best if they stay hidden."

We were both in good spirits as I turned off the Bypass and headed toward my house.

But as soon as I pulled into the cul-de-sac, I stopped the car, and stared at my house.

"What's the matter?" Elly said, her voice tinged with anxiety.

"The house. It's dark."

"It's night."

"I have a lamp that comes on before now."

I inched the car forward.

"Maybe the bulb burned out."

"Yes, maybe that's it," I said quietly.

I pulled in under the carport, cut the engine. Looked around. "Elly why don't you stay in the car a minute. Let me go upstairs first."

"No," she said. "I don't want to stay here. By myself. I'm going with you."

There was no sense in arguing with her. And even with the car doors locked, I could understand why she wouldn't want to sit there alone.

"Stay behind me then," I said.

I saw her look of concern.

We went up the stairs slowly, brushed softly by the damp mist. I got to the door. It was unlocked and maybe had been jimmied. "Uh-oh," I breathed. "Go on back down and be ready to run," I whispered.

She didn't though. It was like she was glued to me.

My cell phone was in my pocket. I pushed the main button and got the what-can-I-help-you-with message. I whispered "Agent Twiddy."

I pushed open the door, reached inside to the light switch next to the doorjamb. The instant I flipped the overhead lights on, the lamp by the telephone also came on.

There he sat, left leg thrown casually over the other.

He smiled, but it was pure evil. "Welcome," he said. "Come on in."

He tried to make it sound friendly; it didn't come out that way.

Chapter Twenty-Eight

He held a slim, long-bladed knife in his left hand and a revolver in his right. My revolver. He held the pistol up, loosely pointed at us. "Found this on your bedside table," he said. There was no hurry to his speech. Just faux casual.

Then his voice changed, became harsher, lost its debonair air. "Sit on the sofa. Both of you." The revolver definitely pointed at us now, and he motioned for us to comply with a wave of the muzzle.

We moved slowly to the sofa and sat, Elly close beside me, our bodies touching.

Neither Elly nor I had said a word. Shocked into silence. We never took our eyes off of him. He slouched comfortably there in the chair, that one leg still thrown over the other. He was dressed in nice slacks, a button down oxford shirt, and loafers that looked expensive, set off with patterned socks. A beige windbreaker coat was folded neatly behind him on the back of the chair.

His eyes. They were the palest gray I'd ever seen. There was a sheen to the skin on his face, which was unnaturally free from any wrinkles or creases. His sandy, somewhat wispy hair was brushed to the side, and seemed to match those eyes.

He looked familiar, and my mind raced to remember.

That smile again, more like a smirk: "It was no problem getting into your little abode," he said. Then a chuckle. "Like you said in one of the classes, a lock is no more than a delaying device."

Then I knew. It came back to me. A memory that had

been lost. He was the one who sat sullenly at the back of the
class, hardly ever speaking a word. His name . . . his name?
"You do remember me, don't you? You should. You
made fun of one of my stories and you wrote about me in
one of your books."
I spoke for the first time, I think. I wasn't sure. "I never
made fun of anyone's writing. And I'm sure as hell I've
never written about you.
I could feel a slight tremor in Elly's body that she obviously tried to control.
"Oh, you tried to conceal my identity in the book. But I
knew. You changed my name, but you made it sound a lot
like mine."
I tried to sound reasonable. "I'm sorry but I can't even
remember your name."
"Sure you do. It's Seymour Demmins III."
Jonathan Clayton had spoken of the guy in the class with
the fancy name that sounded like he'd made it up.
"But, Seymour, I swear I never made fun of anything
you or any of the other students wrote. Believe me. I know
how difficult writing is, and I treat all of it with respect."
His upper lip curled. "Don't try to get out of it. It's too
late now. And you ridiculed me in that book, or tried to." He
uncrossed his legs, leaned forward, a menacing cast to his
face so that his whole countenance took on a different tone.
Doing my best to make my voice even, play down the
hint of pleading in it, I said, "What is it you want, Seymour?
I've never—never knowingly—done anything to you."
"Oh, yes, you have. Yes, you have. And here you are,
sitting pretty with this success as a writer—that could have
been mine if you hadn't ridiculed me. Got your fans here in
this little pond." He gestured with the revolver. "Got this
pretty Miss Elly . . . and her adoring son."
With my palms turned up, placating, peaceful, I started
to rise.
"Sit down," he barked, the soft culture gone from his

voice.

I remained seated, and I could feel Elly's breathing, her shoulder touching mine. "What is it you want, Seymour?"

He looked at me like he might have looked at a slimy insect that disgusted him, his lips partially baring his teeth. A sneer. Contempt. "I'm going to ruin your fancy reputation. I've thought about how to do it for a long time. When you got closer and closer to Miss Elly here, it suddenly occurred to me. A plan worthy of one of your crime stories."

His short laugh made my blood run cold. "A murder and a suicide," he said.

The chilling sound came from his throat. It was supposed to be a chuckle, but it didn't sound like any chuckle I'd ever heard before. The teeth partially exposed again in a leer.

"That will do it." The words slithered out of his mouth. "A murder and a suicide." He nodded his head as if congratulating himself. "We'll see what the town thinks of your reputation then. You'll be ruined."

He gave a laugh and leaned back in his chair. "Of course you'll be dead . . . so you won't experience how everyone has turned against you for this terrible act . . . that you stabbed Miss Elly to death in a rage and then killed yourself . . . but you'll know what it will be like—just before you die."

His entire face morphed into a different cast. The evil leer was there before, but now it became more pronounced. A coldness, a bitter hatred took over the sheen of his facial skin. It was if an invisible set of hands set about silently remolding his face.

He stood, a little unsteadily. He was fairly tall, about six feet, but he appeared much more frail under his expensive clothes than he had when he'd been seated.

Motioning with the muzzle of the revolver, he said to Elly, "Stand up." His other hand remained clutching the long-bladed knife.

Elly tensed but she didn't stand.

I said, "What? Why?"

"I said stand up," he barked.

Elly pushed herself up with both hands; she got to her feet but wobbled visibly. She reached her left hand over to the neck of my bass fiddle to steady herself. She trembled.

I breathed heavily, loud enough for me to hear. I was ready to spring. If we were going to die, I was going to do whatever I could to protect Elly, and attack that son of a bitch. Do some harm to him. I tensed myself on the sofa, ready to spring forward.

In steadying herself, Elly had her thumb on the clasp that holds the neck of the bass in its stand. I saw that and I looked at Elly. She looked back at me, terror in her eyes. She saw me glance at her thumb on the clasp.

I hoped I saw realization in her eyes, the slightest movement of her head.

Seymour saw that I was braced to charge. He aimed the revolver straight at Elly's chest. The hammer was cocked, ready to fire with just a little pressure on the trigger. He was less than six feet away. "You move," he said, "and Miss Elly gets a bullet before you could clear the couch."

I settled back very slightly, but enough for him to see.

It was now time, time to do something, make the effort, even a futile one. I couldn't just sit there. I needed to distract him so maybe Elly could bolt or do something, anything.

Visibly, I shifted to my right, away from Elly, and he immediately swung the revolver and his eyes toward me.

Elly, her jaw set with hard determination, gave my bass fiddle, now freed from the neck-clasp, a strong shove, putting all of her weight into it.

The bass crashed down on Seymour's right side and hand that held the revolver. The neck of the bass hit his shoulder and the gun went off with a thunderous bang there in the enclosed room.

The bass kept falling and Seymour tried to move away

from it, but his legs got tangled up in the body of the bass and he stumbled and sprawled on the floor, landing on his back, arms flung out.

I leaped full-force off the sofa, still in a crouch, knees extended. And I landed with both knees right on his midsection. I heard the air go out of him. My face was close to his. He looked dazed.

His arms looked useless, like the strength was gone, but I knew he would recover quickly.

Elly took two long strides toward him and kicked out hard against the hand that held the revolver. It spun out of his grasp. She stomped on his wrist and then, using the same foot, she kicked him in the face. She kicked him again in the face. Hit his nose and I heard a crunching sound and he yelped but he still didn't have much air in his lungs. It was weak sounding.

He tried to raise his head and I brought my right elbow around, and with all of my strength and weight, I clobbered him in the face with it. I didn't know when, but he had made an attempt with the knife, and it was then, I think, that he slashed at my arm and it started bleeding.

Straddling his chest, I pounded his face with my left fist and then with my right. Back and forth. His head bounced loosely from side to side. He seemed completely out of strength. Losing consciousness.

Elly moved to the other side and kicked at the hand that barely held the knife. It went skidding under the sofa.

"The string on the back of the bass stand," I yelled to Elly. It took a second or two for her to grasp what I was instructing her to do. Then she retrieved the flexible gut G-string draped on the back of the stand and handed it to me.

Rolling Seymour to one side—he was like a rag doll—I brought both of his arms to his back. Whether he was unconscious or just weak, I wasn't sure. But I was taking no chances. With the gut string, I tied his wrists together.

To Elly I said, "911."

She picked up the phone. "No dial tone," she said. These may have been the first words she'd spoken since we came in.

"Unplugged?" I said.

She nodded and looked behind the telephone table to the wall. Plugged the jack back in, listened to the handset, then punched in 911. I heard her talking while I made sure I'd secured Seymour enough. His face was bruised and bloody from the combination of my elbow, fists, and Elly's well-delivered kicks. I realized my right forearm dripped blood on my shirt and onto Seymour's side. I pressed at the cut and saw that it wasn't bad.

Without a word, Elly picked up the revolver gingerly by the muzzle and handed it to me. With an eye on Seymour I began to ease off of him, get to my feet. I felt dizzy; I took a breath and steadied myself. Elly watched me. She stood there hugging herself, trembling. We looked at each other. She cast a questioning look at my arm.

"It's not bad," I said. "You?"

She mouthed an affirmative, an okay.

For the first time I realized Janey chirped loudly. She enjoyed activity.

Then we heard a police siren and saw reflection of blue and red lights on the glass sliding doors as the cruiser pulled up. I head the car doors slam shut and two officers began tromping up my stairs. Another police cruiser arrived and came to an abrupt stop near my carport.

The first two officers came in. They had their hands on their holsters, ready to draw weapons. One of the officers was older and had corporal stripes on his sleeve. The other was young and fresh looking. They took quick appraising looks around.

The older one said, "Put your weapon down, sir."

I realized I still held it, pointed toward Seymour.

I complied, and slowly reached behind me and laid it on the sofa.

Two more officers came in. One of them was a woman. The corporal approached me. "You both okay?" he said. "That arm?"

"It's not bad," I said.

To the newly arrived officers, the corporal said, "Home intrusion."

They began getting Seymour to his feet. He was obviously still almost out of it. They stood him up, and he looked even more frail. Because of the anxiety he had caused us, I guess I had imagined him to be superhumanly strong—instead, he was weak as a kitten.

Someone else came up the steps.

It was Dare County Chief Deputy Odell Wright. I was glad to see him. He took a quick evaluating look at what was going on. He seemed satisfied. "Your cell phone call alerted Agent Twiddy," he said to me. "He called me. Wanted me to check on you." He smiled. "Looks like you've taken care of it."

"With Elly's help," I said. "She's the one who really did it."

She came over to stand close to me.

The corporal addressed Deputy Wright. "Take him away?" He inclined his head toward Seymour.

"Yes," Odell said. "Take him away."

As they started to lead him out, and I noticed that my flexible bass G-string had been replaced by regular hand-cuffs, I stepped forward to speak to Seymour. "I never, ever made fun of your writing," I said. "Or anyone else's for that matter."

He mumbled something. Because of the pounding his face had taken, his words were jumbled, but it sounded like he said, "I could have been a good writer."

Odell stayed with us. He called Balls and reported what had happened.

A little while later I said to Elly, "You ready for me to take you home?"

"Yes. Yes, I guess you'd better." Then for the first time she managed a trace of a smile. "This has been some date, Harrison."

"One I think we'll remember," I said.

Chapter Twenty-Nine

The next morning I was surprised by an early visit from Chief Deputy Odell Wright. With a solemn expression, he trudged up my stairs and I met him at the kitchen door.

"You won't have to worry about whether Seymour Demmins III gets off at trial or not," he said. "This morning when they prepared to take him to Raleigh they found him dead. He hung himself. Tore up a sheet, tied one end around his neck and the other end to the window's bars."

I sat at one of the chairs by the dinette table. I motioned to Odell to sit but he remained standing. We were silent for two minutes at least. Then we must have talked a bit but I don't remember. I guess I went over a lot of it all in my head and I tried my best to accept that now, at last, it was really and truly over.

Before Odell left, I asked, "Why Raleigh?"

"They'd linked him to that killing of a mother who had the young son a couple of months or so ago."

"He also killed a totally innocent young woman in Paris," I said. I stood and rested my hand on the edge of the kitchen counter near Janey's cage. "He was going to kill Elly and me. Try to make it look like murder and suicide,"

Odell nodded, then smiled, "Agent Twiddy can relax now. He's been real worried about you."

After Odell left I called Elly. She had stayed home from work. I think Mabel had already telephoned her with the news about Seymour Demmins III. My emotions were mixed about him. He was evil, I knew, or at least he had become evil. I doubted he'd started out that way; something had been missing I guess from the beginning maybe he really did want to be a writer, a good one, and he was consumed with the knowledge that he'd never make it, and that I had achieved a degree of success. He couldn't accept that.

But Seymour Demmins III had become a killer, Harrison, don't forget that.

There was no way I could forget it.

It would take a while, I knew, for the shock of what we had been through to make Elly feel, well, normal again. But she would. I came to realize in Paris and certainly here at my house in the confrontation with Seymour that she was indeed, as she described herself, one tough Outer Banks gal.

Friday night she had invited me to her house for dinner that her mother wanted to make for us. It would be good to be there, getting back to normal, see Mrs. Pedersen and young Martin; then, after dinner, I was determined to sit with Elly out on the porch swing in the golden evening there in Manteo, and finally—without fail and no more delays—to give her that ring.

CPSIA information can be obtained
at www.ICGtesting.com
Printed in the USA
LVHW040851300720
661936LV00002B/300